Will I E
Betrayal on t

Terry E. Mills

Copyright © 2024 Terry E. Mills All Rights Reserved

Dedication

This is dedicated to those who witnessed my life long labor;

Who indulged me; who listened; who read and reread my writing.

To those who offered support and loved me through the process.

To those who taught, encouraged, and accompanied me.

Thank you!

Terry E. Mills

2024

Acknowledgments

My thanks to Val, Sherry, Hilda, Kim, Shea,

Women who see strengths and celebrate triumphs;

Strong women who walk a path of empowerment every day;

Who unselfishly and enthusiastically invite others to join the journey.

Terry E. Mills

2024

Contents

Dedication 3

Acknowledgments 4

Chapter One... 7

Chapter Two 11

Chapter Three 15

Chapter Four 19

Chapter Five.. 23

Chapter Six.. 29

Chapter Seven... 35

Chapter Eight 41

Chapter Nine... 45

Chapter Ten 47

Chapter Eleven.. 51

Chapter Twelve... 57

Chapter Thirteen... 63

Chapter Fourteen.. 69

Chapter Fifteen 75

Chapter Sixteen... 77

Chapter Seventeen.. 83

Chapter Eighteen 85

Chapter Nineteen.. 91

Chapter Twenty 95

Chapter Twenty-One 101

Chapter Twenty-Two.. 107

Chapter Twenty-Three 113

Chapter Twenty-Four 119

Chapter Twenty-Five 125

Chapter Twenty-Six 129

Chapter Twenty-Seven 135

Chapter Twenty-Eight 141

Chapter Twenty-Nine 145

Chapter Thirty 149

Chapter Thirty-One 153

Chapter Thirty-Two 157

Chapter Thirty-Three.. 161

Chapter Thirty-Four.. 165

Chapter Thirty-Five 167

Chapter Thirty-Six 171

Chapter Thirty-Seven 173

Chapter Thirty-Eight... 177

Chapter Thirty-Nine 183

Chapter One

Although a fist was clenched at my side, I listened purposefully as the words rolled off his tongue. I nodded and tilted my head, with raised eyebrows, as if his explanation was illuminating. To him and to the onlookers in this crowded room, I was undeniably caught up in his self-professed victory. Breaking momentarily from internal anger, I secretly applauded my Sunday night performance. When he looked at me, he spoke as if he perceived my intrigue was genuine. That is what I wanted: To revel in the fact that he was blind to his own ignorance, and the reality of this moment eluded him. I wanted to betray him – as he had betrayed me – and many others. My satisfaction loomed in the unsuspected nature of this premeditated betrayal. It was, after all, created by a deep-seated need for reprisal. The sleeping giant of hatred had been awakened in the midst of his evil. I wanted justice. Who had I become?

The library smelled of cigar smoke and cologne. Champagne was served from silver trays resting on the palms of numerous caterers. Their white shirts, black ties, and vests added a professional touch. Their demeanor was subservient. They did not make eye contact with or speak to the guests, who were from the Merit Society's A-list. The waiters were instructed to be "invisible." I watched Morty infiltrate the waiter staff and pour champagne into flutes as he observed the elite. He liked pouring the liquid gold, and he had a special interest in one young server. He glanced at me from across the room. An impulse lifted the corner of my mouth, almost allowing a smile to escape. I gathered myself and moved toward the terrace. Michael finished his oration, and his adoring audience, drunk from champagne and taken in by his power, shouted accolades. He grabbed my wrist and growled, "Let's get some air, Carly."

Outside the doors of the library, the moonlight flooded the patio. The stone wall was wet from rain, and the puddles reflected the moon's glow like tiny moonbeams shining upward. Michael was handsome in this light. If one were looking out from inside – this was a perfect scene for a love story. The air was cool and damp. The perfume of wet roses wafted through the garden.

"I thought I told you to wear the black dress," Michael snapped.

I looked down at the gorgeous, red, form-fitting, and shimmering Versace.

"I thought this would be a nice surprise." He tightened his hold and narrowed his eyes. "You're hurting me," I said.

"You know I don't like surprises," he hissed. "Do what I tell you to do. Must I remind you?" He took my hand and placed it on his black tuxedo pants. I felt his manhood. "You are a bad girl. You know what happens to bad girls!"

I pulled my hand away and walked into the library. My heart was pounding, and my chest was tight. Michael watched me go; I felt his penetrating and unforgiving gaze. I knew what came next.

I nodded as I re-entered the library and quickly walked in the direction of the stairs. Morty subtly acknowledged my return. He dropped the powder into a flute and met Michael at the door with champagne. Michael's eyes lingered on me as I climbed the stairs. He took the glass from Morty's hand.

"Dismiss the guests, with my apologies," Michael said angrily. "Give them all a bottle of Champagne for their inconvenience."

He gulped down the Champagne and handed the flute to Morty, who slipped it into his jacket pocket. Michael pushed his way through the guests and ascended the stairs.

The tightness in my chest was comparable to the tightness of his engulfed flesh. It was difficult to breathe. Michael pushed the door open, revealing my naked breasts as my dress fell to the floor. His actions were predictable, and resisting was futile. He slammed the door and grabbed me by the elbows. He slapped my face and threw me on the bed. He covered my mouth with one hand as he retrieved his engulfed flesh with the other. He thrust himself hard inside me. His hand stifled my scream.

I remained completely still as I anticipated his next thrust, but there was nothing more. His body, went suddenly limp. I bore the full weight of him. He was motionless. I rolled him off me. The momentum carried him to the floor with a thud. Lying still, I breathed a deep sigh. I was trepidatious and apprehensive; was he breathing?

I waited ten minutes -- as Morty had instructed. I watched Michael's body for signs of life and saw none. I began screaming, "Help! Help! Help!"

I remained naked as planned to garner sympathy and divert suspicion. Others came running. First, the maid, Shelby, followed by Dalton, a member of Renee's staff; then Michael's father, George Candiss. Pandemonium ensued, and 911 was called.

Someone yelled, "Get the Doctor. We need the Doctor."

I sobbed into silk sheets as Michael's father covered my naked body. I let out a tortured cry.

Michael's father shouted, "Where is that, Doctor?"

As Michael's skin turned purple-blue, the doctor came into the room.

"Please, stand back and give me room." He felt for a pulse. He listened for breathing. He drew back and delivered a hard blow to the chest. He delivered two breaths and began CPR. He counted out loud, "1, 2, 3, 4," up to 30, then delivered two more breaths. Michael's body was lifeless. The ambulance arrived, and the medics took over as they loaded Michael onto a gurney and whisked him away. Doctor Mortimer turned his attention to me. I was now quiet on the bed, as if out of my body. George asked if Michael was going to live. Dr. Mortimer shook his head and sighed, "It is doubtful, George. I'm sorry. I'll follow right away and do what I can." Michael's father left the room, with Dalton close behind. The doctor said, "Shelby, get some ice for Carly's face."

Dr Mortimer took my pulse. He looked around for other observers. He said, "How do you feel, Mrs. Candiss?"

I remained downtrodden and distant. Shelby brought in a small ice pack, wrapped it in a washcloth, handed it to the Doctor, and left the room. Morty applied the ice to my face and said, "It's important for you to rest, my dear. I'll go to the hospital, and we will contact you soon."

I blinked both eyes. Morty excused himself and ran out. Michael's mother, Renee Candiss, entered the room, disheveled and inebriated.

"What happened?" she inquired. She stood braced against the wall to avert a fall. Her words slurred as her personal assistant, Gwen, and the cook, Emily, held onto Renee's shoulders. "What happened?" she repeated loudly.

I lifted my downward gaze, "I think Michael had a heart attack," I said.

Michael's mom shouted, "Is he dead? Is my boy dead?"

"I don't know," I answered.

Renee was assisted by her staff as she staggered from the room. I heard her wailing as she went down the stairs and out the front door. Was it over? Was my betrayal complete?

Alone in my room, I stretched out on the bed. I sunk into the thick, white, down comforter, and I took a deep breath. I tried to relax and shake off the surreal nature of what had just occurred. For the first time since my marriage to Michael ten years ago, I felt safe. I had lived in fear too long. I sighed deeply. I thanked God and Morty for my life. Perhaps, with Michael dead, I might live. I reveled in Michael's demise at the hands of Morty/Dr. Mortimer – my friend and co-conspirator. At that moment, I had no regrets. I would show my gratitude for his courageous efforts on my behalf. I was indebted to him for my freedom and my future. The shackles of evil had been removed. Emotionally and mentally exhausted, I fell fast asleep.

Chapter Two

The door opened around midnight. It was George Candiss. He awakened me with a gentle touch to my lower back. He knelt at the bedside and sadly said, "He's gone, honey. Michael's gone." I let out a guttural sob and gasped. Was it all a bad dream? George gently touched the bruise on my cheek. He put his arms around me. "Dr. Mortimer says it was a heart attack." George held me tightly, too tightly. He wept into my nightgown, "A man can't live the way Michael lived for very long," he said. "I did my best...rest assured that everything will be fine. You'll see," he said. Tears fell from his eyes and rolled down his tanned and weathered face. His deep wrinkles and furrowed brow added age to his features.

George bore the burdens of his betrayal, a long marriage to an alcoholic and excessive woman, as well as a son whose indiscretions were a constant cause of embarrassment and expense. My father-in-law was motionless as if lost in the embrace of someone else. I felt compassion for him. I began to cry-out loud. He loosened his embrace and stood to leave.

He nodded, "You'll see, Carly," he said. "Everything will be fine."

I was relieved when I heard the door close behind him. The heaviness of the night seeped into my body and carried me to escape in slumber.

The morning light crept into the room from the East window. The sheers glowed as if ignited by fire. I rolled over and looked at the light. I felt free. I wondered how life would punish me. I wondered if there would be punishment at all or if the world would thank me for ridding it of an evil man. I felt no remorse or sadness. On the contrary, I felt light, calm, and relieved. I was faced with the task of showing a different face to the family. I would construct a façade to enable me to get through the next few months. I needed to carry out a deceitful portrayal. They must never know the truth. I deserved the entitlements of a grieving widow for surviving the abuse at Michael's hands and the embarrassment of Michael's whims. My future was a powerful driving force and further justification for my actions.

Shelby lightly knocked twice on the door. She came into the room carrying a tray. She wore a mournful expression.

She said, "I'm so sorry, ma'am, for your loss. I am shocked."

I nodded and kept my gaze down and despondent. She nervously rattled on about Michael's unexpected death. She talked about his powerful personality as she poured coffee and added cream. She placed a napkin in my lap as I sat up. Our eyes met. She was aware that I knew of her affair with Michael like I was aware of the others.

She said, "Let me know if there is anything you need."

I held her gaze but did not reward her with any sign of forgiveness. I wanted her to feel shame. My usual anger returned as she exited. I set aside the covered tray in my lap. I had lost my appetite.

I moved to the terrace for my coffee and poured a second cup. Renee, who had been sequestered in the den all morning, nursing a vengeful hangover, called upstairs.

"Carly, Dr Mortimer is here to see you, dear." Morty started his ascent up the stairs. Renee asked, "Doctor, can you help me with this pounding headache? Since my son's death last night, it has been severe."

Without turning to witness her response, Dr. Mortimer said, "A hair of the dog, Renee."

She waved her hand with a dismissive gesture and returned to the den. Dr. Mortimer stepped onto the terrace. Always aware of the many eyes in this house, Morty kept his smile small and compassionate. He held me with an appropriate embrace. He whispered, "Are you feeling better?" I nodded and rubbed my cheek on his warm neck, which slightly smelled of sweet cologne.

"Did you notice?" I asked, "I have only one bruise on the morning after a party. That's a first."

Morty sat down and poured himself coffee. He spoke in a low tone, "The first of many firsts, Mrs. Candiss."

Dr. Mortimer continued, "I provided the certification of your husband's death to the state, Mrs. Candiss. I faxed over the necessary paperwork this morning. Due to symptoms, drug use, and extensive cardiac history, as well as his engagement in strenuous sexual activity after drinking to excess, I saw no need for an autopsy. George and Renee agreed, and the M.E. declined the case. The cause of death is Myocardial Infarction or heart attack. The state will file the death certificate and authorize cremation. That will take about a week. Once the family receives the death certificate, Michael's beneficiaries can petition the insurance company for life insurance benefits."

I sat quietly.

"Thank you, Doctor," I said.

Watching his tongue and minding his facial expressions as if the walls were listening and watching, Dr. Mortimer said, "My condolences, ma'am. I am so sorry for your loss. It is an unexpected tragedy."

Dr. Mortimer left the house after checking in with my in-laws. My mother-in-law, who had followed the Doctor's advice and indulged in some morning gin, was feeling better, albeit bereft. My father-in-law was on the phone with the Houston offices. George was business-like and focused as he managed the situation. He considered the "next in line" candidates to assume Michael's duties. There was also the call to Joanne. She was a woman in her late forties. George set her up in an apartment years ago. The only requirement was her company during monthly visits to Texas. He paid her generously. She would remain on the payroll. George would see to that. I knew little about her. I found myself wondering if monetary compensation was worth abuse and emotional torment. I wondered that for myself, as well. Joanne would keep the apartment. Mourning, in my opinion, was doubtful.

George and Renee joined me on the stone terrace. George's secretary, Maxine, with tablet in hand, waited for instructions. George began, "We will have the public services at St. Mark's for your mother-in-law." Renee wiped tears from her cheeks. "Michael's ashes will be interred in the family plot next to his grandfather and great-grandfather. George handed me a list. There will be a reception here after a private graveside service. Go through the guest list and approve those considered for an invitation. You were privy to his opinions out of the public eye. We will leave those decisions to you. Of course, family members, Joanne, obligatory attorneys and bankers, will remain on the list." Nodding somberly, I glanced at the top of the list and noted Dr. Mortimer's name. George concluded, "Dignity is most important, Carly. We must keep our heads."

Maxine, who had been at George's side for nearly 15 years, took Renee by the hand. Sobbing bitterly now, Renee was inconsolable. Maxine shot a look at George as she led Renee downstairs to be handed off to Gwen. George stepped toward me. I picked up the coffee pot and poured him a cup. I invited him to sit with me. I expressed the complicated nature of my relationship with his son.

"George, you have wonderful staff and supportive friends; you are a lucky man. Maxine is strong and capable. I am sure she will be a comfort to you."

Leaving an awkward pause, I waited for George's reply.

"She is a dear. I count on her for too much."

I nodded. "She has become a confidant over these years, yes?"

George's face grew stern. He took a long sip from his cup. "Yes, a confidant of sorts. One can never have too many of those, Carly, and discretion is key."

George left the room amid the assumption of infidelity.

Chapter Three

The service at St. Mark's was as beautiful as the rustic church. There was standing room only for those paying their respects. The green grounds and gardens were the perfect backdrop for the spectacle of the wealthy. The priest's eulogy was paid for by Renee. She got her money's worth. According to the Priest, Michael was already sitting at the "Right Hand of God," an accomplished human who was home at last. My uneasiness was palpable. This had been the longest nine days of my life. I thought about how the rich could buy anything for the right price. Anything except the love and loyalty of those they deceived, invalidated, and abused. I wondered how -- in the Church -- his accomplishments in life justified Michael's wicked behavior, which would now be forgiven in death.

I was suffering from the need for distraction. I counted the women with whom Michael had affairs as they approached to pay their respects. He told me about them, sharing sordid details prior to the sexual encounters in our marriage. It was his version of foreplay. He kept a list of conquests. That list was part of his tormenting threats. He enjoyed the power he wielded with cruelty. I counted four single women and six married women. I counted three teens, all of whom were seduced and consented to his advances but cost George half of the family's income to keep quiet. Michael was an evil man. He was a poster child for narcissism, sociopathy, and sexual addiction. I was happy to rid these people of him. I would not ask for forgiveness. The real challenge was to justify vindication beneath tears of guilt.

As the church bells rang outside of St. Mark's, the crowd shuffled out into the drizzle of light rain. I caught a glimpse of Joanne. She was supported by George's driver, Marc, who was seldom seen outside of the limo. She hung heavy on his arm. She held a white handkerchief to her face. Her black hat had a sheer black veil, and her auburn hair fell just below her ears in a stylish bob. Mascara was smeared under her eyes, and her lipstick was pale like her face. Poor dear, she looked older than her age. I felt sorry for her. She could make no claim that would allow the comfort of the crowd. I wondered why–or how–she could look or be–sad. It was unfathomable that any woman could miss the pure evil that Michael was. I would never understand her apparent loss. Was it an act?

Dr. Mortimer took my elbow and accompanied me from the church to the waiting limo. He held the umbrella over my head and raised the collar on his raincoat. George and Renee were in the first car with their staff. Dr. Mortimer and I followed in the second car. After we were dry inside, he asked, "Are you holding up, Mrs. Candiss?" He offered me a bottle of water.

Between sips, I replied, "I am coping, Doctor."

I watched Dalton's eyes in the rearview mirror. He seemed disengaged; caution was advisable.

"Mrs. Candiss, are you sleeping all right? Are you eating?"

"Yes, Doctor," I responded.

Morty slipped a small piece of paper under my hand. I glanced at it without making an obvious movement to pick it up.

"We'll be together soon."

I nodded, folded my fingers around the note, and dropped it in my purse with my Kleenex. Dr. Mortimer escorted me to the graveside.

A small group of mourners gathered and reaped the societal recognition of the invited. I caught sight of Joanne being ushered away as the family approached. The coffin sat on wide canvas straps above the grave that would encompass it for eternity. It was a highly polished dark-wood and housed the urn. The headstone lay beside the grave. The inscription read: "Beloved Son and Husband." The ultra-gloss on the casket reflected the dark blue sky and the white clouds that dropped their drizzle as if shedding tears. I presumed the sky was mourning the desecration of the earth by an evil man's ashes. Hatred for Michael burned in my heart. I longed to move forward toward redemption. I needed to stay ahead of the consuming guilt that pursued me.

Morty worked the crowd, shaking hands and sharing hugs. He offered condolences to Renee and George, as well as their staff. He thanked the priest for his words in the church service. I was moved to the right of the Priest at the head of the casket. I was breathing deeply and praying to make it through this masquerade. I looked up and caught Morty's gaze. His expression was caring. He nodded in my direction as if acknowledging my internal struggle. I was glad he was there.

The Priest began, "Lord, please accept Your son. Grant absolution of his sins that he may enter Your Kingdom unscathed by the errors of this life. Forgive him as the father forgave the prodigal son on his return home. Open your arms and receive him, Amen."

The crowd replied, "Amen."

Grief-stricken Renee stepped forward and put a rose on the casket. I fell to the wet ground.

I awoke in my bedroom. Dr. Mortimer was leaning over me and removing a wet towel from my forehead.

"Hello, Mrs. Candiss," he said.

Renee was fanning herself. She leaned forward in her chair and stood up, "Are you feeling better, dear?"

I attempted to sit up but was seized and held down by dizziness. "What happened?" I squinted at George and Renee, who looked at Dr. Mortimer.

"You fainted. Too much stress, excessive humidity, and an abundance of emotions. It was too much to take in, I suspect. You just lost your husband to sudden death. You need rest," said the Doctor as he exited the bedroom and went into the bathroom.

"Yes," George said, standing and taking Renee's hand. "She is going to be all right. Let's see to our guests and let the woman rest."

"Please, take your staff with you," I pleaded.

At once, Dalton, Gwen, and Maxine jumped to their feet and followed the grieving parents out. Morty came into the bedroom from the bathroom with another cool hand towel. He cautioned me to tell him if I felt unstable so he could stay close.

He asked, "What happened, Carly? What were you thinking or feeling?"

I sat up and began to sob real tears. What had I done? Who was evil now? Had Michael's faults been forgiven and left me cursed by hatred, condemned by my actions?

Morty put his arms around me. He said, "There, there, Carly, darling. Don't worry. It's almost over." He leaned me back again, resting my head on the pillows. He put the cool hand towel on my forehead. His touch was reassuring. He said, "Rest." He stayed until I fell asleep. That is all I remember of the day we buried my wretched husband.

Chapter Four

I woke in the morning to clinking ice in Renee's glass as she opened the sheers. She saw my eyes were open. With a degree of pretend surprise, she said, "Oh, you're awake! I know it's a little early to be drinking but with Michael's death and all . . . !"

I raised my head and asked, "What time is it, Renee?"

"Quarter past eight," she said. "Have some coffee. You haven't eaten in days."

"What? What day is today?"

"Thursday," she chirped.

"But Michael's funeral was Tuesday," I said.

Concern swept across my face. Renee handed me my robe, "Whatever is the matter, dear? You needed your rest." She encouraged me to wash my face, "You'll feel better."

My legs were weak as I approached the sink. I looked in the mirror and peered at the reflection of someone new: A widow and a murderer.

Renee rang for Shelby, who brought up breakfast and opened the terrace doors. For September, the air was warm and balmy. The rain had passed, and the grass glistened green below.

"Dr. Mortimer checked on you yesterday, dear. You slept through his visit. He made it a point not to disturb you. He is the nicest man, isn't he? I will never understand Michael's loathing for that nice Doctor."

It was clear that Renee's gin was working. After I used the bathroom, washed my face, and brushed my teeth, I was more prepared for Renee's pleasantries. Out on the terrace, Renee was just beginning to eat her breakfast. She poured my coffee and added cream.

"Thank you, Renee."

She raised her glass, "Liquid courage, my dearest; liquid courage. You might want to add a splash to your coffee."

Renee was summoned to the downstairs office phone. I reflected on the day and a half I slept through. I wondered if that was what death was like. I sipped my coffee and savored the deep flavor. My senses seemed awake. My phone rang. I noticed the remaining weakness in my legs as I walked across the room.

"Hello."

"Hello, Carly, this is Judy. Are you ok, my friend? I have been worried about you."

"I missed you at the graveside," I said.

"Did you and Roger get the invite?"

"Yes, I'm sorry," she said. "Something unexpected came up." Judy got a call on the other line. "Carly, I need to call you back, OK?"

"Yes," I said, and hung up.

I went back to my breakfast and felt better after eating. The sun climbed higher in the sky. Almost two weeks had passed since Michael's death. It was a blur. I turned on the shower. The water warmed my heart and soul as well as my body. I could feel life pouring back into me. I let the warmth run over my head and down my back. I lingered. My senses had been awakened in some odd way. Maybe this feeling was the reason serial killers carried out their crimes. Life was enhanced; colors, odors, and flavors were more pronounced. Or was it the realization that Michael was gone and the abuse was finally over? I would not suffer again at the hands of an evil man. Were my actions justified by the torment? Would I, too, be forgiven someday?

I towel-dried and pulled on my favorite pair of leggings, some mid-calf, waterproof boots, and a blue frock. I gathered my long hair into a ponytail and was grateful to be a brunette in the long line of blondes who Michael entertained. I applied a slight touch of mascara and a swipe of blush. Sitting at the marble vanity and looking into the 16th-century stone-framed mirror, I assessed myself to be appropriately plain. I tugged at my wedding ring and decided to leave it on. Shelby came in and went about cleaning.

"Will you take a ride this morning, Mrs. Candiss?"

"No, Shelby, I think I'll walk today."

"Do be careful, Mrs. Candiss. You are weaker than you know. You have been in bed for two days after a traumatic experience."

"Thank you, Shelby. I will be careful, and I won't go too far." I admitted to myself that she was a nice young woman, albeit seemingly naïve.

As I descended the stairs, I took in the beauty of the home I lived in for ten years. When we first married, we stayed in Vermont, but soon after, Michael's parents insisted we move into their second-story suites. In the beginning, I thought it was altruistic. I soon realized Michael's proximity gave George the opportunity to keep tabs on his wayward adult son and run interference when poor decisions were made. I was aware that Michael's presence in his father's home was a necessity rather than a luxury. It was a life of opulence that was forced upon me due to my husband's propensity for trouble. I smiled to myself. Being surrounded by wealth and beauty was a reasonable price to pay for freedom.

The 60-acre estate was full of class and color. The trees were mature, and their stature was impressive. The pastures surrounded by cedar fencing were plush and rich. The gardens were colorful and aromatic, as well as functional. We willingly ingested vegetables from the "North End," which was overseen by Renee, although her real passion was roses. The paved roads ran through the estate from the guard shack in front by the main house, past the pastures, to the barn and corrals, the breaking pen, the guest cottages and storage facility, then out to the back of the estate, where there was a second gate and guard shack. The guard shacks contained state-of-the-art surveillance equipment which was monitored by four guards who had been employed with George since the union riots and mob involvement. The entire estate was surrounded by a solid block wall topped with spiked, black iron bars. George was somewhat hypervigilant. Wealth was its own paradox for which one must pay a high price.

As I ambled down the stone walking path just off the paved road, I heard an engine approaching. It was George in his white, convertible Mercedes.

"Hello, dear. It is good to see you up and out."

"Thank you, George, I felt the need for a walk."

"I suppose you don't want to hop in and see the new foal?"

"No, thank you. I'll catch up."

"OK," he said and sped off.

George had two mares who were hopefuls for the mile race -- on grass -- at Merit Downs. Opening day was just two weeks away, and the buzz had already begun. Michael's, and now my gelding, "Handsome Fellow," looked good for the six furlongs. He was a former favorite, now moving up in class. George was sure that the youngster would have no problem with the new "in-class" competition.

He said, "I'd bet my life on it."

Renee was constantly asking George to refrain from using that expression. Renee felt like it was "asking for bad luck." George very seldom listened to Renee's superstitions.

As I approached the barn, I saw George's Mercedes parked next to Dr. Mortimer's red BMW convertible. What was he doing here? Why had he not checked in with me? I shook off the paranoia that permeated these grounds. When I entered the barn, Dr. Mortimer greeted me with a subdued smile.

"How are you feeling, Mrs. Candiss?" he asked.

He took my hand and kissed my cheek.

"I feel tired, Dr. Mortimer, and somewhat weak."

He nodded thoughtfully. "The stress of Michael's sudden death is too much to endure. Rest is key and will be important as your body, mind, and heart are healing."

I saw a glint in his eye.

George appeared from a stall and said, "Listen to the doctor, dear. He is a well-paid consultant around here who has a good eye for a horse."

George and Morty shook hands, and George asked, "What brings you here today, Doctor?"

"Just checking in on my patient, and I wanted to see that foal, George."

Chapter Five

Morty and I followed George into the stall. I caught a glimpse of the Estate foreman, Raul. He was a strikingly handsome man with a strong, athletic build. He had worked for George since the Estate was established fifteen years ago. He was a hand with a horse, knew agriculture, and was a strong and confident leader. He saw to the upkeep of the grounds, the care of the stock, the maintenance of the gardens, and the management of the security staff. Raul resided in one of the guest houses. I wondered what he would do with his extra time now that Michael was not harboring one-night stands for Raul to cover up.

As I stepped into the stall, I saw the sac and placenta of a mare who had given birth just a short time ago. She was licking and nibbling at the ears of a newborn whose coat was not yet dry. I gazed upon a thing of beauty, a black foal, lying in the straw, not able to stand on his lean and unsteady legs. The men were watching enthusiastically and George handed everyone a cigar.

"Welcome to the world," George shouted. "He is a handsome one."

"He is," I agreed.

"What will you call him, George?"

"Well," he said, "In anticipation of his birth, I picked out a name last night. I hope you won't mind, Carly, and if it's OK with Dr. Mortimer, I will call him 'Missing Michael.'"

I left the stall, but not before witnessing the look that passed between Raul and Morty. George followed me. I began to sob. Guilt was gnawing at me. How did I expect to do this? I killed my husband. I belong in jail. Would I be free, or would guilt be a life sentence? George took me in his arms and held me as I wept.

"Carly, dear . . . all of this will pass; life will go on. We need time to collect ourselves."

I was hesitant to trust George but found myself resting comfortably in his embrace. His concern seemed and felt genuine.

Morty said, "Let me take you back to the house, Mrs. Candiss."

George agreed, "Yes, Doctor, a good idea."

Morty put his arm around my waist and guided me to the car. As he helped me into the passenger seat, I whispered, "What have we done?"

Morty closed the door and walked to the driver's side. He started the engine and replied, "What we had to do, darling . . . what we had to do."

The day was getting warm as we drove back to the house. Renee was out front directing her staff. She explained the seating for the party opening day. She wanted all the decorations up by the day before. She wanted the caterers dressed in the colors of the horse's post positions, and she wanted the liquor served from "trophy goblets." She insisted that the trainers, Jockeys, and stable hands were at the head of the table.

She said, "They deserve recognition, win or lose."

She greeted Dr. Mortimer with a kiss on the cheek.

"What's in that tea?" he asked.

"Just a little sunshine," she answered with a wink. She turned to me, "Oh dear, you've been crying."

I wiped the tears away and acknowledged her powers of observation despite too many spiked iced teas.

"Yes, Renee, I've been crying."

"You must gather yourself, dear," she said.

Morty said, "Let's get you upstairs, Mrs. Candiss."

Up in my suite, I fell into Morty's arms with a deep sob leaping from my chest.

"Oh, Morty," I gasped. "What will I do?"

He held me tightly and whispered, "What will WE do? You are not alone."

I pulled away from his arms and said, "I forgot – I have you and Raul, right?"

Morty dismissed my possessive comment. "You're tired, you need rest." He helped me out of my boots and disappeared into the bathroom. He returned with my robe.

"Morty, will everything be all right?"

"You have my word," he said. He turned his back as I undressed and put on the robe. I got into bed, facing away from him. "Now close your eyes and rest – don't worry."

He massaged my shoulders, upper back, and ribs, coming dangerously close to my breasts. I felt the tension leave my body. I turned to him and asked, "Is there something I should know about between you and Raul?"

"Rest," was his reply.

"Carly, Carly . . . wake up, dear." I felt as if I was coming up from underwater. Renee, Gwen, Dalton, and Shelby were towering over me. The doors were open to the terrace, and it was sunny outside. "Carly," Renee said, "Are you ok, dear?"

I sat up slowly.

Shelby took my hand and swung my legs over the side of the bed. "Did you have a nice rest, dear?"

"Yes. Yes, I did," I answered.

I squinted at those who were staring at me, "What are you staring at?" I asked.

Renee replied, "You dear . . . why did you cut your hair?"

Gwen went into the bathroom and returned with a mirror.

"Why did you cut your hair, dear?" Renee asked again.

I looked in the mirror and gasped. My long, beautiful hair was gone, replaced by a shoulder-length cut, curling inward. "Oh no. Who did this?" I shouted.

"You did," Renee said. "Shelby discouraged you, but you insisted."

I looked at Shelby, who was nodding. "That's true, Mrs."

I wondered what else had transpired while I was unaware.

Renee had coffee brought to the terrace. Still, in my robe, I was foggy-headed and perplexed. Shelby brought out my sunglasses, and I was grateful. The sunlight was overpowering. She put slippers on my feet and left us. As Renee poured the last smidge of rum from her flask into her coffee cup, she said, "The Mayor is coming over to discuss the charity auction on opening day. He is anxious to know who the MC will be now that Michael is gone?"

"I thought the mayor was coming on Sunday? I asked.

Renee raised her eyebrows and replied, "Honey - today is Sunday."

"It can't be," I argued.

"It is Friday or Saturday morning. Oh Renee, what is happening?"

She put her hand on my shoulder and rang for Shelby to bring up breakfast. She said, "and ask Dalton to bring a bottle, Carly and I need a drink."

I sat silent as tears rolled down my cheeks.

"Renee, when did I cut my hair?"

"Yesterday, dear. Don't you remember? I woke you and asked if you wanted to walk to the barn to see the foal. You declined, and I went down alone. When I returned, Shelby told me what happened. When I came upstairs, you were asleep again. I called Dr. Mortimer and left a message, but he didn't call back."

"Has he been here in the past two days?" I inquired.

"No. I haven't seen him since Thursday," she said. "Unless my liquor intake deceives me. You know how forgetful I can be in the afternoon. Do you want me to ask the others?"

"No. No. That's all right, Renee."

She excused herself. "I'd better get to work. There is lots to do before opening day, eat something dear."

Overcome with hunger and uncertainty. I indulged in an over-filled plate of eggs, bacon, biscuits, gravy and potatoes. I called Morty. There was no answer; I left a message asking him to call me as soon as he could. After breakfast, I opened my closet. Many of my clothes were gone. I rang for Shelby. I caught sight of myself in the mirror. I looked terrible and oh, my hair, my beautiful hair. I turned on the shower. I teetered to one side, dizzy and weak from excessive time in bed. I put my hand on the wall to brace myself. Shelby came into the bathroom.

"Ma'am?"

"Shelby, what happened to my clothes?"

Shelby was confused. She said, "Ma'am, we donated them yesterday. You said they reminded you of Michael, and you wanted new things. We ordered quite a bit from that website you like, 'Elite Clothing.' You ordered two new dresses for me, as well. You insisted."

I dropped my robe to the ground and stepped into the shower. Shelby picked up the robe and left the room with a sigh. I closed my eyes, put both hands on the shower stall, and let the warm water run over my face. I needed to talk to Morty.

Chapter Six

I pulled on a pair of jeans and a T-shirt and blew dry my hair. I would have to learn new ways to style my hair or cut it off completely.

Renee called from downstairs, "Dr. Mortimer, dear."

I walked to the door. Morty's look of surprise was obvious, "Nice hair, Mrs. Candiss, it suits you."

He was carrying an unlit cigar.

"Been out to the barn?" I asked.

With a look of embarrassment, he replied, "Yes. Checking on the foal."

"I bet," I replied smugly, suspicious of his frequent visits to the barn.

"You haven't forgotten George and I co-own that little lad, have you?"

"Yes," I admitted; I had forgotten.

Morty jarred my memory, "George and I invested in that mare three years ago at auction. I liked her coloring, sturdy confirmation, and temperament, but I lacked the capital."

"Oh yes, I remember. You asked Michael for a loan. He told you that you shouldn't be a thrill-seeker at the racetrack."

Morty nodded, "Yes, now you remember."

I was aware of Morty's unfortunate gambling outcomes. He liked long shots.

"How can I help?" he asked.

"I am having memory issues," I said.

"Issues?" Morty repeated.

"Yes. I seem to have lapses. I am missing days, events, and situations. I am forgetting my own actions, case in point, my hair. I don't remember cutting it."

A look of deep concern crossed Morty's face. "When did this start, Mrs. Candiss?" I began to hyper-ventilate. I was struggling to catch my breath. Morty grabbed me by the shoulders. "Calm down, Mrs. Candiss. Breathe deeply, breathe, breathe . . . Let's figure this out." I was trembling as Morty eased me into a chair. "You appeared to be fine, although tired when we spoke yesterday," he said.

"Were you here yesterday, Doctor?" I asked.

"Yes, I came in before I went to the barn. I saw Renee leaving to see the foal. You were awake in bed but wanted to stay in bed. You said you wanted to go through your closet. I didn't stay long."

I didn't remember his visit at all. Apparently, neither had Renee – for entirely different reasons.

As the panic passed, Dr. Mortimer said, "Now start from the beginning, Mrs. Candiss. Tell me what has happened. This may be a temporary response to trauma, but we need to get to the bottom of it as quickly as we can."

I told Morty the entire story. He explained that the memory lapses could be stress-related blackouts or PTSD. I knew what he called "stress" meant guilt from killing my husband. He was satisfied that I expressed no audio or visual hallucinations, which he said could indicate something altogether different. Dr. Mortimer was clearly worried. His prescription, for now, was rest.

As he left the suite, he said, "I am making an appointment with a neurologist."

I sat in the sun on the terrace and tried to relax. It was impossible. I thought a ride might be nice. I hadn't ridden my bay since the day Michael...well, since the day of his death. I pulled on my riding boots and walked downstairs. Dr. Mortimer was in the den speaking with Renee. I forced a smile and joined them.

"What are you two up to?" I asked.

Renee had a look of worry.

Dr. Mortimer said, "There's my patient; up and about, are you?"

"I thought I would take a ride." Renee cautioned, "Oh dear, do you think that's wise? Better wait till you're feeling stronger."

"I'll be fine," I said.

"Mrs. Candiss," Dr. Mortimer said, "It may be a good idea to listen to your mother-in-law."

I turned to the Doctor, "I'll be fine," I said sternly. "A ride will do me good;

it's been a while since I've ridden these grounds." I proceeded to the barn, and Dr. Mortimer left through the front gate.

When I got to the barn, Raul was closing his phone. I heard him say, "Sure thing." He reached out to shake my hand, "How are you, Mrs. Candiss?"

"I am doing as well as can be expected, Raul. I'd like to take a ride. Will you saddle the bay, please?"

"Right away, ma'am." Raul brought my bay, "Miss Molly," into the barn from her stall. She was a beauty, although developing a slight hay belly. She whinnied, and I nuzzled her. She was a lady: Strong and sound, yet soft and eager to please. I watched Raul brush her before putting on the saddle blanket and saddle.

"No bit," I said. She prefers a hackamore. Raul nodded. "Raul, you and Dr. Mortimer are good friends, right?" He did not look up.

"Yes, Mrs. Candiss, Dr. Mortimer referred me for this job 15 years ago. We are long-time companions. The Doctor ran interference when Michael and I had our disagreements, which were many. Your husband was hard on me, ma'am."

I nodded in agreement, "He was hard on all of us."

I mounted my girl and gently leaned forward. It felt good to be in the saddle. Molly responded to my lead and walked slowly out of the barn. Raul hurried ahead to open the gate. I kicked my heels, and Molly picked up her pace into a neat, girlish trot. I kicked again, and she changed her gait into a smooth and comfortable lope. She was a nice seat; an enjoyable ride. I missed her. We loped the grounds of the estate, enjoying each other's company. I went over recent events, in my mind, trying to piece together all that had happened. I rode to the far end of the Estate. The last guest house was out of view from the main road. I saw Morty's car under the carport. I trotted Molly to the back door.

Morty stood inside the large picture window. His short black hair, neatly combed and pushed back, glistened from the gel. His sculptured features and green eyes smoldered beneath subdued masculinity. I gasped and dismounted, feeling moisture in my loins. As I entered the cabin, Morty took me into his arms and kissed me deeply. He pulled me into him, holding me firmly and close. I kissed him gently, passionately. He sighed my name, "Carly." We stood in close embrace, happy to shed emotional chaos. I basked in the safety of his arms. He said, "Darling, it's over. When an acceptable amount of time passes, you won't be expected to stay here. We can appear to serendipitously fall in love. George and Renee will give their blessing, and our new life will begin in Vermont."

I wanted to believe him. I let out a long moan and begged Morty to make love to me. I needed to feel closer to him. He said, "Not now, darling. These grounds have eyes, ears, and a vendetta. We must exercise caution." Morty walked me out where my horse was waiting. He gave me a strong leg-up. I looked directly into his eyes.

"I need your help, Morty. This is harder than I imagined." I wondered what happened to that sleeping giant that was empowered and awakened the night Michael's fate was placed in my hands. Where had that determined woman gone?

As I made my way back to the barn, I was able to feel some relief. I started to feel almost normal. I let Miss Molly have her head, and she broke into a full run across the estate. She was deliriously happy. She had the speed of a thoroughbred and the strength of a quarter horse. She was magnificent. Michael was right when he picked her; she was the perfect horse. As I arrived at the barn, I saw Raul and George entering with the Veterinarian. One of the stable hands took Molly and exchanged her hackamore for a halter.

"Thank you, Jim," I said.

"She's wet," he said.

"I hope I didn't overwork her."

He hooked her up to the hot walker, "I'll cool her down, Mrs.," he said.

I walked into the stall with the mare and new foal. The Vet, Dr. Jonah Silvers, was explaining something to Raul and George.

"Is everything all right, I asked?" Jonah took my hand and kissed my cheek. He offered condolences.

"Thank you, Jonah," I said.

"It must be difficult to deal with the sudden death of a young man," he said.

"Yes. It was a shock."

I was unnerved by Raul's gaze. Did he know something? George sensed my nervousness and reassured me that Jonah's visit was "routine."

"Jonah," I said, "Can I have your cell number? I am lost without Michael's contacts, and I can't find his phone."

Jonah took out a business card and wrote down his personal cell. He was the best man at our wedding and, most likely, Michael's only friend. I thanked him and left the barn, "Good to see you, Carly," Jonah called after me. I headed for the main house on foot.

Chapter Seven

The sky was clear above, but clouds hung on the horizon. Rain would be coming in by evening. I felt the urge to go to town. Merit City was surely missing me and my spend-thrift spouse. I decided to shower and go in and see Judy at the salon about my new hairstyle. When I got to the house, Dalton was holding a box, and Renee was on a ladder.

"Shouldn't you be on the ladder?" I asked Dalton. He rolled his eyes and handed Renee an ornament.

"Now, Carly, just because I tip the bottle every now and then, don't suggest I can't manage a ladder, dear."

"Never, Renee," I replied.

"I would never suggest that."

I winked at Dalton, and we all chuckled. I made my way upstairs.

The house phone was on the dresser in my room. There were three lines, and I could see one was in use. I wondered who was on that line. Renee and Dalton were out front. Shelby was in the Master suite upstairs; I heard the vacuum. Emily, the cook, was retrieving vegetables from the garden when I passed, and George was at the barn. I had not seen Marc since the funeral, and that left Gwen. She was Renee's personal assistant and made most of Renee's calls. I had to ignore the desire to pick up the phone and listen. Instead, I called the salon. Judy was glad to hear my voice. She told me she would make room in her schedule whenever I arrived. She was excited.

She said, "We need to catch up. How are you, Car?"

"We'll talk later," I said.

I turned on the shower and shed my clothes.

After my shower and the donning of fresh, clean, comfortable clothes, I went downstairs and started out the front door. Renee, who was slightly tipsy, inquired into my plans.

"I'm going to see Judy. I need some help with this hair."

Renee slurred, "I'll have Dalton drive you."

"No, Renee, that won't be necessary. I have a perfectly good Camry in your garage that hasn't been driven in a while."

Renee said, "Doctor's orders, dear."

I asked, "Why, Renee?"

"Oh, he's being over-protective. He doesn't want you out alone. Remember, you passed out . . . and your memory . . ."

Renee instructed Dalton to bring the car around. I felt that further protest would lead to a more difficult departure; I acquiesced.

Dalton smiled, "Thank you, ma'am," he said as he opened the car door.

We pulled up in front of the salon. Judy ran to the car, flung open the door, and hugged me. She squeezed me for a long while. She burst into tears, "I'm so glad to see you, woman!" she shouted. She took hold of my hair and asked, "What happened, love?" she squeezed me again.

Judy was my one true friend. I did not realize until that moment how badly I needed to see her. I began to sob. Judy grabbed me by the hand like a four-year-old and led me to the back. She sat me at the breakroom table and held my hand as I sobbed uncontrollably. She stroked my hair and kissed my head.

"Oh, sweetie," she said, "Just let it out."

The tears kept coming. I was rendered speechless. She stood by and loved me, like the long-time friend she was.

I swigged down a cup of coffee with a bagel as Judy offered ideas and opinions about my hair. She said, "I could just shape the cut you gave yourself, and we could see what that looks like?"

Exhausted, I agreed. Judy's young beauty school student and salon tech, Frances, washed my hair. I sat back with my eyes closed and my head over the sink while the moisturizer soaked in. I listened to the radio and found myself humming along. I was calm and cleansed by my tears. Judy was finishing another client's hair and carrying on about a bad tip she received the week before. Judy was, among other things, a comedian. Everyone in the salon was laughing out loud.

The woman in Judy's chair said, "Remind me to give you a good tip."

The tech replied, "I know, right?"

Judy trimmed, shaped, and styled my hair. A very different look was born. Judy said, "You know, it suits you, Carly."

I looked at myself in the mirror, and tears began to fall again.

In Judy's tender way, she said, "Honey, you've been through too much. The town is buzzing about Michael's death, the funeral, and the upcoming opening day."

"And you don't know the half of it," I said.

"Then you'll have to tell me," she said.

"Spend the night, Roger won't mind. He'll be asleep by ten, anyway. Come home with me, Car."

After Judy finished my hair, we all cleaned the shop. Judy said, "Fran, you can take off, honey. Thanks for your help. Just count the tip jar, take half, and I'll see you at nine in the morning."

Fran did as Judy said and disappeared onto the streets of Merit. Judy called Roger and told him she was on her way and was bringing a guest for dinner. There was so much I wanted to tell Judy . . . that I could not.

I dismissed Dalton with little argument on his part. I told him to tell Renee that I would be with Judy and not alone at all. I asked him to retrieve me at Judy's shop the next morning at ten. He agreed and left for the Estate. Judy locked the salon door, and we got into her yellow Mustang.

"I love this car," I said.

"You should," she said.

"You helped me pick it out."

"I remember," I said. "The salesman at the dealership tried to convince you to cheat on your husband for a better deal."

We were still laughing when we went into the house.

Roger was at the kitchen sink wearing an apron. He hugged me, kissed my cheek, and said, "We missed you, missy. I am sorry to hear about Michael, but he got what he deserved if you ask me."

"Roger!" Judy shouted.

"It's all right, Judy," I said. "Roger is probably right."

An uneasy quiet consumed us briefly until Roger said, "I have made you two queens a gourmet dinner."

I looked in the oven and spied an extra-large, ultimate veggie pizza, and my mouth watered. Judy opened three beers and we all sat down at the kitchen table -- old friends. I missed this connection. But I couldn't deny that Michael loomed large . . . like he always had. Would I ever be rid of him?

Roger took the last swig of his third beer and surrendered to fatigue. We hugged, and he kissed me goodnight. Judy followed him upstairs. She handed me a microwave popcorn bag and told me she would be back downstairs before it was done popping.

"Get us another beer," she said.

I put the popcorn in the microwave. I was lost in the wonder of the moment. How can this feel so normal? Where had this feeling of well-being been? Then I remembered: It was stolen by an evil man who kept me away from my friends. I was his property and could only see others when he was out of town.

Judy returned to the kitchen just as I poured the popcorn into bowls. She opened the beers and took her bowl to the couch.

She asked, "TV or deep and drama-driven conversation?"

I chose TV. We turned on the funniest program we could find and laughed at the benign humor. We tried to find ourselves or people we knew in the personalities of odd characters. Once our beer and popcorn were gone, we settled into conversation. Judy asked about Michael's death and about the family. She asked if I heard from or about Joanne. I filled her in on all I could. I told her of Michael's anger prior to his physical and sexual abuse as well as his death. I told her about my blackouts. Judy listened intently as I shared Dr. Mortimer's care and concern.

Judy said, "Dr. Mortimer hated Michael, Carly. Dr. Mortimer was berated and invalidated by Michael on a regular basis. He knew more than anyone about Michael's cruelty. I'm surprised he tried to render CPR at all. I'm just happy Dr. Mortimer has such a good friend in Raul."

I was taken aback. Did the entire town know of Morty's relationship with Raul? Was it only a secret to me? Was there more to it than I realized? Were my feelings of trepidation warranted? I felt my spirits sink. I was working on the courage to tell Judy about my fondness for Morty when I realized she was asleep. I turned off the TV and covered her with a blanket. I went into the bathroom and told myself to stay in the comfort and calm of Judy's home and not let panic overtake me. I tried not to let my mind wander into a place of foreboding. I wanted to tell Judy what I had done – how Michael died because of my actions and Morty's expertise. I wanted to confess.

I brushed my teeth with a new toothbrush I found in a package under the sink. I changed out of my clothes into a nighty Judy left for me. I prayed for forgiveness, and I thanked God for Judy and Roger. I looked at my new hairdo and marveled at Judy's talent. I noticed that my face had changed. I had lost weight. I had a new and sophisticated look. Indeed, I was a new person – with whom I wanted to become acquainted.

Chapter Eight

The alarm went off at 6:30 am. Roger came downstairs in his blue plaid boxers and put on the coffee. Judy rolled over and begged to sleep ten more minutes. I sat up and greeted the day with a new enthusiasm. There were people who loved me: Morty, Renee, George, Jonah, Judy and Roger. I convinced myself that, if they knew, none of them, except Renee, would fault me for what I did . . . what Morty and I did. I ventured to believe I would be found innocent if the truth ever found its way to the court. I was the true victim. Roger said goodbye, kissed Judy, and left for work.

After a breakfast of English muffins and cereal, Judy and I headed for the salon. We made a stop at Starbucks to further indulge our caffeine cravings. We purchased three seasonal drinks. One to share with Fran and for each of us to try. We turned down main street, and a firetruck whizzed by with siren blaring. When we approached 3rd and Main, we saw a commotion in the street.

Judy gasped, "It's Fran."

I looked in the street and saw the firemen working to secure Fran to a backboard and load her into a waiting ambulance. We pulled over and jumped out of the car. Fran was unconscious.

"What happened?" Judy asked.

"She was hit by a car ma'am," the paramedic replied.

"Who . . . where . . . is the car that hit her?"

"They didn't stop; it was a hit and run." A gentleman close by shouted, "He ran her down; I saw it. He ran her down."

Judy jumped in the ambulance. I followed in Judy's car.

I entered the emergency department's waiting room at Memorial Hospital carrying two coffees. Judy was in the back with Fran. It was crowded, and the air was stale and still. Tearful people with worried looks paced the floor. Families were gathered. I drank my Starbucks, trying to remain calm, and hoped Fran would be ok. What a horrible thing. Who could hit a young girl and leave her for dead in the middle of main street? I dialed Morty's number.

"Dr. Mortimer," he said.

"Morty," I barked, "something terrible has happened."

"Carly, darling, where are you?"

"I'm at Memorial Hospital."

"Are you alright?" he asked.

I told Morty about Fran. "I'm on my way."

Judy came out of the E.R. She had a terrible look on her face – "Carly," she said, "Fran is in a coma. I need to call Roger and reach Fran's parents; they live in Cator. I'll need her information card from the salon. Carly, can you call Roger and tell him what's happened. I'll run to the salon, put a sign in the window, and come right back here."

"OK," I said.

My first call was to Dalton, who was on his way to the salon. I told him not to come for me and to let Renee know I was with Judy. I refrained from saying what was going on.

I looked at contacts in Judy's phone. I pushed number 2, which was listed as "Roger." He answered right away, "Did you tell her yet?" he sounded tense and terse.

"Roger," I said, "this is Carly."

Roger stuttered, "Oh Carly, where's Judy?"

"There's been an accident," I said.

Roger screamed, "IS JUDY OK?"

I reassured him and explained what happened. He didn't ask how Fran was. I told him Judy would return from the shop soon.

He said sternly, "Have her call me as soon as she returns."

He hung up. Has Judy told who . . . what? I drew in a deep breath.

Judy got back to the hospital just as Morty arrived. She was surprised he was there. I said, "I called Dr. Mortimer, Judy."

Morty shook Judy's hand, "I'm here to help if you'd like. I have privileges in this hospital."

Judy seemed apprehensive. After a long pause, she said, "I called Fran's parents from the shop. They are on their way. They are driving from Cator, so it will be about an hour. I would think, Dr. Mortimer, that they would appreciate any assistance, information, or support you could offer. All we know for now, is that she was hit by a car and is unconscious.

Morty excused himself and disappeared behind the double doors of the E.R. Judy watched him go. She took a long look at me.

"Roger wants you to call him." Judy dialed the phone and walked across the room. It was apparent that a confrontation was taking place. I heard her say, "I said I'll call you later."

She came back to our seats.

"What was that about?" I asked.

"Carly," Judy said, "I'm sorry I didn't bring this up last night, but it was not the right time. Now is not the right time either."

"Go on," I urged. Judy shifted her weight and pushed aside her bangs. She took a long drink from her coffee, "Carly, there is a rumor that Michael did not die of natural causes."

"WHAT? What are you saying, Judy?"

"Well," she began, "Someone started a rumor among the jockeys and stable hands that Michael was killed. He had plenty of enemies, Carly. The accusations are that there were reasons for the cremation and no autopsy. People are suspicious of Dr. Mortimer."

Judy sat back in her chair, scanning my face for reaction.

I looked at Judy in disbelief. I asked, "And what do you think?"

She replied, "Well, I, for one, wouldn't blame you if YOU killed him. As far as I am concerned, Michael is where he belongs – with the devil!"

I became short of breath. I was aware of the sweatiness that was washing over my body. Judy grabbed my forearms and said, "Carly . . . honey . . . are you ok?" I could not speak or breathe. Judy called out to the hospital staff, "I think we need help here!"

Morty entered the waiting room and immediately saw the panic on my face. He put his arms around me and whispered, "Breathe, darling." The tension in my muscles loosened. "Breathe," he repeated, "Breathe." He asked an RN to bring oxygen. He held a mask to my face and let the oxygen flow in, encouraging me to relax. "You're fine, dear." Judy watched as Morty talked me into calm. She witnessed my recovery as panic subsided. But Judy saw something else.

Fran's parents came into the waiting room through the ER doors. They were in tears and hysterical. Dr. Mortimer introduced himself and offered his input and services, which they gladly accepted. Fran's mom hugged Judy tightly. We all listened as Dr. Mortimer explained, "Fran is in an induced coma for her own protection. She suffered head trauma, a concussion, and several broken bones. They need to take control of all functions due to the acute nature of her injuries and the pain she endured. In a few days, as the pain and swelling subside, her life-support will be withdrawn, and we are confident she will recover quickly. There is no evidence of brain damage. Her neuro tests are negative. So, you see, the bad news -- is basically good!"

Everyone gasped in unison, and Fran's parents, escorted by Doctor Mortimer, went back to see her.

Chapter Nine

Judy and I were finishing our coffees, when two police officers entered the room. I recognized one of them from the night of Michael's death, Detective William Roder. He came to the house with the paramedics and spoke with George. The other officer, I knew from the track in general, but mainly from the Candiss' private box. His name was Hector, and he knew Michael. The officers approached and introduced themselves. Hector offered condolences. They wanted to ask Judy some questions about Fran. Judy and Detective Roder went outside. Hector told me that he was looking forward to opening day. He said he'd miss Michael's advice. Michael often gave "racing tips" to our men in uniform. They didn't seem to mind that it was technically illegal. Officer Roder and Judy rejoined us. The officers headed into the E. R. to see Fran's parents and speak with the doctors.

Hector said, "See you on opening day, Mrs. Candiss."

Judy excused herself. She seemed alarmed.

"I have to call Roger," she said.

She went outside again. I picked up our coffee cups and some other pieces of trash around the room and carried them to the bin. I looked through the windows on the double doors and saw Morty talking with Hector. They were laughing, and their body language was friendly and relaxed. Of course, it made sense that they were friendly since they both frequented the box at the track. Why was I feeling nervous, paranoid, and suspicious? I wondered if those feelings were the result of my sins? Did murderers feel these feelings forever? Was paranoia part of the murderer's psyche for life? I guessed that was a question to which I would eventually learn the answer. Suddenly, I was aware of my exhaustion. When Judy returned, I called Dalton and asked him to come and take me home.

Judy and I held each other's hand. We had a lot to discuss but sat in silence for a long while. I stood to leave and explained that fatigue had gotten the better of me. I needed to lie down. Judy asked if I was coping, OK? She asked if, by any chance, I missed Michael.

I shook my head, "No," I said. "I suppose I should, but I don't – am I bad?"

Judy shrugged, "I never miss a migraine and Michael was a big headache."

We both forced a smile. I told Judy I'd come into town another day, and we could finish our conversation. I asked her to update me on Fran.

"If you see Morty, will you tell him I've gone home?"

Judy raised an eyebrow and replied, "Morty?"

I corrected myself, "Dr. Mortimer."

"I will," she said.

I walked out the door to find Dalton was waiting at the curb.

Dalton opened the door, and I fell hard into the seat. I was weak. He asked if I wanted to go straight home?

"Can you stop at Pete's?" I asked.

"I think we all need some Jamoca Almond Fudge, don't you?"

"Yes, ma'am," he replied.

Pete's was empty. Ellen, who was in the back as we came in, met us at the counter.

"Oh, Carly," she said, "I have been thinking about you since the funeral. How are you, child?" She bent under the counter and came to me with a robust hug. "I am so sorry for your loss."

"Thank you, Ellen." I pointed to Dalton and said, "Renee has the whole house looking after me." Dalton nodded. "Can we have two gallons of ice cream?" I asked.

"A gallon of Jamoca and, what else do we need, Dalton?"

Before he could answer, Ellen said, "Dalton will want fresh strawberry. Ain't that right, Dalton?"

He grinned and answered, "Yes, Miss Ellen, Strawberry."

Chapter Ten

After we finished our ice cream and I had filled Renee in on the day's events I went upstairs. I was weak from fatigue. Shelby came in with some fresh towels and turned down the bed.

"Are you feeling all right, Mrs. Candiss?" she asked.

"Fine, Shelby," I answered.

"There is mail for you, ma'am. I put it on your desk."

"Thank you, Shelby," I said.

"Will there be anything else, Ma'am?"

"No, Shelby, thank you. I'll see you tomorrow."

I turned on the shower. The water was relaxing and forgiving. If I could live there, I would be at peace. It was soothing as it poured over my tired body. The shower temporarily filled my need to be cleansed. I thought of what Judy said, and I wondered about her hatred toward Michael. I wanted to tell Morty, but it could wait till tomorrow. I wondered how Fran was.

Getting into my nightclothes, I remembered the mail. I went to the desk and looked out the window. I was glad Shelby had not drawn the curtains. I picked up my mail and opened the terrace doors. A cool breeze carried leaves onto the terrace. The first signs of Fall were fast upon us, and opening day was just a week away. I poured myself a glass of water and sat down, facing the grounds. It was a beautiful night. I looked through condolence cards and junk mail. I dropped the mail on the table and closed the terrace doors. I pulled the curtains closed but caught a glimpse of a shadow standing beside the garden downstairs. I paused in front of the window and blinked in case it was my imagination. It was not. There was someone there.

I ran downstairs. Renee pursued me as I went by the den, "Whatever are you doing?" she slurred as she stumbled after me. Once outside – I called out, "Who is there?"

Renee was standing beside me, "Carly, you mustn't run out in the dark. Who are you looking for?"

"There was someone out here, Renee. I saw him – just a minute ago from the terrace."

She looked around, "All the more reason not to run out, dear. I don't see anyone."

"Neither do I," I said.

We went inside. Renee was perplexed, "Who did you see, Carly?"

"I couldn't tell," I said.

Renee called the guard shack, "Ralph, has anyone out of the ordinary come on the grounds tonight? I see, and have you monitored the grounds on camera? I see; nothing unusual. OK. Thank you, Ralph. Please keep a lookout, won't you? Carly thought she saw someone outside the main house. Yes. Yes, I suppose it could have been one of the stablehands or groundsmen. However, it is quite late. OK, Thank you."

Renee hung up and shrugged.

Renee and I went into the den. Dalton was printing address labels.

"Hello, Mrs. Candiss," he said.

Emily was stuffing envelopes. She nodded. "Where is Gwen?" I asked.

Renee poured us a cognac and said, "Where she wants to be."

The tone in her voice was secretive. Dalton shrugged and continued his work. Emily did not respond. I noticed Shelby's absence.

"Carly, darling, let's have a drink to better days."

We clinked our glasses and sipped the Remy Martin Louis XIII Magnum. Truly an exquisite experience. Renee raised her glass and said, "One of the best Cognac's ever made: Matured in oak casks. You just drank two months of Emily's wages."

Emily looked up and rolled her eyes, "Better see you up to bed soon, Mrs."

Renee patted Emily's head, "Yes, but don't call Shelby. Let her have an evening. Emily, Dalton can finish up. You can see me to bed."

I kissed Renee and returned to my suite. I looked out on the grounds again. A chill ran through me.

As I settled into bed, my mind raced. How much can a mind process? The degree of energy that it took to hold my composure each day was exhausting. I wondered how Morty managed so well. Did he have experience of which I was unaware? Nothing seemed to ruffle his feathers. That was one of the traits I loved most about Morty and that Michael found most repugnant. Michael used to say he could "Never get a bead on him." Michael would intimidate Morty to try to get a response. Michael failed miserably. Morty's defense was not to react, no matter what. Morty sustained years of abuse at the hands of Michael. It dawned on me that Morty was, perhaps, as relieved about Michael's death as I was.

Eventually, I fell asleep and slept late in the morning. When I woke, I went to the window and looked down on the grounds. Weighing heavy on my mind was the identity of the man outside last evening and why he was there. I wanted to go and have a look around. I made my way out front. There were footprints. They looked like round-toed boots with tire tread-like soles, work boots, maybe. They were not cowboy boots or dress shoes. That eliminated several people right away. It was not Morty or Raul or any of the stable hands or jockeys.

George called to me from the main house. I joined him on the downstairs patio. I told him about the man I saw and the footprints, "Carly, the man you saw is one of my men," he said.

"He is looking after you. I worry about your safety. Michael had a lot of enemies."

"George, why didn't you tell me?"

"The fewer people who know, Carly dear, the better. No one knows, except Raul and the security team."

I thought about Morty's insight and warnings. "How long has he been watching?" I asked.

"Since the funeral," George answered.

Immediately, I remembered my meeting at the guest house. Was I seen with Morty?

When I went back to my suite, I was feeling anxious. I phoned Morty and left a cautious message: "Dr. Mortimer, this is Carly Candiss. Can you please come to see me when you can? Thank you." I sat on the terrace and looked at the mail I dropped on the table last night. I opened the condolence cards, read them, and noted who they were from. Despite Michael's abhorrent personality and all that transpired over the past ten years, I found the cards to be sincere in their warm wishes and thoughtfulness. I felt supported by a community that, until now, I assumed tolerated me because I was Michael's wife. Of course, that was all Michael allowed me to believe.

Shelby came in with brunch.

"Would you like something to eat, Mrs. Candiss?" Shelby placed the tray on the table in front of me.

"Yes, thank you," I said.

"It is a beautiful day, ma'am," Shelby said.

"It is," I agreed.

"Shelby, can you tell me why you slept with my husband?" I asked.

Shelby's face went flush.

"Ma'am?" she asked.

"Why did you participate in a sexual relationship with my husband?" She fell into a chair, visibly shaken. "Oh, come now, Shelby," I said quite cruelly. "You don't have to feign remorse. You know I knew."

"Everybody knew, ma'am," she said. "Michael didn't keep his conquests secret. He bragged about them."

I asked again, "Why, Shelby?"

She looked directly into her lap and began to cry. "For my job, Mrs. Candiss. He would have fired me, otherwise and black-balled me in this town."

I was shocked, "You slept with my husband for this job?" I asked.

She nodded and explained. Shelby confided details of which I was unaware, but I had the feeling she was still holding back.

After my conversation with Shelby, I had a lesser degree of guilt about what I had done. I did not realize how far-reaching was the reign of Michael's terror. I did not know how many women he intimidated, threatened, and manipulated to suit his sexual whims. Shelby enlightened me. I was glad and sad to get the details of Michael's cruelty. I was sorry for the women, and I forgave Shelby. She was a slave to Michael's power. I would ask Renee to give Shelby a raise and a vacation.

Chapter Eleven

Renee was in the den when Dr. Mortimer arrived. I heard the bell ring and started downstairs. When I arrived in the den, Renee was telling Morty about last night. Morty looked interested and concerned.

He heard me coming, "Hello, Mrs. Candiss."

"Hello, Doctor," I replied.

Renee poured three glasses of lemonade and took out a flask. She asked if either of us wanted "a little dash." Dr. Mortimer and I declined. Renee added three dashes to her own, "One for each of us," she said, smiling.

Renee answered her ringing phone. Dr. Mortimer and I went out to the patio, where George was talking with Maxine, who was taking notes. George stood up and shook hands with Dr. Mortimer, "That foal is looking fine, Doctor," he said.

Morty nodded, "Yes, and he's already a runner." George introduced Maxine. Dr. Mortimer shook her hand, "Of course, we've met, Maxine, it's nice to see you."

I nodded to Maxine, who nodded and said, "Mrs. Candiss," as she left the patio.

George invited Dr. Mortimer and I to join him. George's phone rang, and he held up one finger and motioned for us to sit. I asked Morty if he would "Walk with me?"

George's phone call consumed him. He barely noticed when Morty and I left. Once out of earshot but still in a whisper, I told Morty about last night. I told him about my conversations with George and Shelby that morning. Morty kept hold of his reactions and emotions. I could see he was listening intently.

I asked, "Do you think George's man saw us in the guest house?"

Morty looked around; he looked behind and ahead, to the West and to the East. He said finally, "I imagine, Carly, we are being watched remotely, as well. We must be careful, but we need to let our affection show in small ways. Our relationship should not look forced but real."

I took hold of his arm.

"How is Fran?" I asked.

"She is doing fine," he answered.

"Carly, tell me what happened that day?" I told him all I knew.

"Hector said something," Morty hesitated, "He said it looked like an intentional hit and run."

"That's what a man at the scene was shouting," I remembered. "He said she was 'run down.'"

"Why would anyone want to run that girl down?" he asked.

"I don't know. I just met her the day before. She works for Judy at the salon. We were on our way back there when we came upon the accident. It was awful."

Morty put his arm around my waist, but this was not for the cameras. I knew he loved me. I could feel it.

"Careful, Dr. Mortimer," I cautioned.

He smiled, and we continued to walk. "Did I tell you how much I like your hair, Mrs. Candiss?" he asked.

When we arrived back at the house, Dr. Mortimer informed us that my appointment was scheduled with the neurologist, Dr. Nadal, at Community Hospital. It would be the Monday after opening day. Morty explained the importance of follow up considering the memory lapses and fatigue. It was good news, and I was relieved. He left to go to the barn. His foal was a new and positive focus. I struggled with his relationship with Raul. I fought off possessiveness and jealousy. I did not know how deep the relationship went or if there was anything about which I should worry. We all have special people in our lives; we all need close friends. For the moment, I chose to believe that the man who killed for me, loved me enough. I found resolve in that: Morty's love had to be real.

I called Judy at the salon. No answer. I called the number again. Still no answer. I called Roger's cell. No answer. I thought that was odd. Renee appeared in the doorway.

"Carly dear, I need to go to town and pick up my dress for opening day. Do you have one, dear?"

"No, Renee, I do not. Remember, I seem to have donated my clothing?"

"Yes," Renee said, giggling.

"Perhaps it's the first time I remember something you do not."

We both shared a hearty laugh. "Dalton is waiting for us," she said.

"Let's go and try to have some fun."

The three of us drove into town.

Dalton dropped us off at the Waymark Inn. It was the nicest restaurant in Merit and close to the racetrack.

"I am famished," Renee said. Eddie B. met us at the door.

"Mrs. Candiss and Mrs. Candiss – so nice to see you both. Your table is waiting. Wine or whiskey?" he asked.

"Whiskey," Renee replied and winked at me, "Wine, please, Eddie – red."

As we were seated, all of Merit's elite watched Renee's grand entrance. She waved, threw kisses, gave hugs, and provided colorful entertainment. But Renee was very much the grieving mother. Eddie returned with the whiskey and the wine and explained the day's specials. Renee chose the surf and turf. I chose the salmon. We had a delightful meal.

After lunch and one too many whiskeys, we went to the dress shop on Main and 6th. I was surprised that Dalton was not waiting out front.

"Oh," Renee said, "I'm sure he'll be at Pete's till later on."

"Does he like Strawberry ice cream that much?" I asked. "No," Renee said, "But he does like him a lot of Miss Ellen." I felt like I was awake for the first time in ten years. How did I know so little about the people who surrounded me every day of my life?

Renee tried on her maroon, brown, and gold floor-length dress with a flowing skirt and short sleeves off the shoulder. She had chosen the colors of Fall. Celia made a few minor adjustments.

"I'll pick it up tomorrow," Renee said. I was standing in the mirror in an exquisite, ankle-length, backless, form-fitting, burnt orange, satin dress with elbow-length sleeves.

"Perfect for the Fall," Renee said.

"You don't think it's a bit much?" I asked.

"Nonsense, dear. You look lovely as ever. Celia – let's add beaded, black trim to the hem, down the front of the V-neck, and to the sleeves," Renee said.

"Perfect," Celia responded.

"That will break up the orange," Renee said as she threw back a gulp from her flask.

Outside, the beautiful day was fading.

"Let's get to Pete's," I said, "and find our ride home."

"Oh, no, no, Carly," Renee said. "I'll call Dalton and tell him we're ready. We must not let on that we know his whereabouts. It would embarrass him terribly. We'll wait at Hattie's."

Renee called Dalton and told him we were ready and he could pick us up at Hattie's coffee shop. We went in and ordered three espressos to go. When we exited the shop, Dalton was waiting at the curb. I handed him a coffee and noticed the sweet smell of soap lingering on his body. He had taken a shower. His visit with Miss Ellen must have been a good one. I smiled to myself.

"Good for him," I thought, "good for him."

As we turned into the Estate and stopped at the guard shack, Dalton got out of the car.

"What's going on?" I asked.

Renee, who was feeling no pain, replied, "He's just getting the tapes, dear."

"The tapes?" I asked.

"Yes, dear, the videos of the Estate grounds for the previous day. Dalton picks them up and leaves them on George's desk for review in case the guards report anything out of the ordinary. He also watches the horses in the corrals and pastures. He notifies Raul if he sees any signs of sickness, lameness, or bad behavior."

"Oh," I responded, "Does he watch personnel, visitors, employees and such?"

"Of course, dear," Renee said, "If Michael taught your father-in-law nothing else, he taught him that few people can be trusted."

For more than one reason, I felt guilty.

As we moved toward the house, I saw George's limo coming toward us in the opposite direction, leaving the Estate. I saw Marc, George's driver, at the wheel. I had not seen him since the day of Michael's funeral when he was supporting Joanne.

"I haven't seen Marc in a while, now," I said.

Renee looked toward George's limo and said, "He's been out of town, darling, in Texas. He got back this morning."

"Oh?" I asked, "And how is Joanne?"

"Let's not concern ourselves with trifles, my dear; We must never concern ourselves with trifles," Renee answered.

Chapter Twelve

I was happy to lie down and fell asleep quickly. Unfortunately, my dreams were violent and disturbing. I blamed the wine, the salmon, and the caffeine too late in the day. I woke to my phone ringing. I looked at the time – 0630.

"Hello?" Judy was sobbing, "Carly, can you come over? It's Roger."

I sat straight up, "What's happening?" I asked, "Is Roger ok?"

"I don't know where he is," Judy said as she continued to weep.

"What are you saying?" I asked.

"He didn't come home last night. I haven't seen him since he left for work yesterday morning. No one knows where he is, Carly."

"I'll be there as soon as I can." I rang for Shelby, who came up right away. "Shelby, can you ask Dalton to take me into Merit, please? I just need about 30 minutes."

"Yes, Mrs. Candiss," she said.

Dalton was at the front door when I went out. George was having coffee on the patio. I explained I was going to Judy's and there was concern for Roger. He seemed alarmed and asked me to update him. Dalton asked if I wanted to stop for coffee, and I agreed that would be nice. We were almost at Judy's front door when Morty called. He was surprised that I was up and out of the house. I shared the phone call with Judy. He called to see if I knew about the opening day celebration.

"Did you know that Renee planned a tribute to Michael?"

"No. I didn't know," I said flatly. "It makes sense and seems appropriate," I said.

"Yes," Morty said, "All things considered, it's quite like Renee. She was blind to Michael's flaws. I just wanted you to be prepared. Let me know about Roger."

Judy was waiting outside. She was smoking a cigarette. We hugged long and hard. I handed her a latte and asked, "Since when do you smoke?"

"These are Roger's," she said. "I started smoking five minutes ago when I lit this one."

We went inside. I asked her to tell me everything. Judy said, "Roger has been acting strange since Michael died. You know Carly, Roger asked me to hire Fran 'for a friend.' When I asked him why, he wouldn't say. He is keeping something from me."

"What?" I asked.

"I can't figure it out. When he heard rumors about Michael's death at work, I told him to call you. He said, No. I don't know why he wouldn't. He is super upset about Fran's accident, but we all are, right?"

Judy and I waited at the house in case Roger came home. She called the feed store several times. He was not there. We called both hospitals. He was not in either. I called the police station and asked to speak with Hector. When Judy left the room to use the bathroom, I called Morty to give him an update. Judy was despondent. She was full of dread.

"This is so unlike him," she said.

"Where could he be, Carly?" I was perplexed. None of this sounded like Roger. He is a devout husband who loves his wife. He is a hard worker. He has lots of friends and no enemies of which I was aware. Judy began to sob, and I held her close.

The doorbell rang. I was glad to see Hector, but I didn't like the look on his face.

He said, "Hello again, Mrs. Candiss."

I said, "Hello."

"Would you step outside, please?"

"Sure," I said.

The other officer brushed by me; he was with Hector at the hospital. Hector told me to turn around.

"What's going on?" I asked.

Hector spun me around and handcuffed me.

He said, "You're under arrest for the murder of Roger Stiles." Judy screamed.

She came to the door. Hector said, "I'm sorry, ma'am. Officer Roder will take you to the station."

I begged, "Judy, you know I didn't do this. I would never harm Roger."

Hector read my rights and said, "Your gun was found at the scene."

"I don't own a gun," I said.

Judy dropped to the ground. I broke loose of Hector and touched my cheek to Judy's. "I'm so sorry. I love Roger, too. We'll find out what happened, I promise. Call George Candiss. Tell him what's happened. Let him know I've been arrested, please!!" Judy nodded through heartbreak and tears. Officer Roder tried to comfort her as he helped her gather her things and get into the patrol car.

I was booked into Merit County Jail and put in a holding cell. They took my shoes, my jewelry, my purse, and, of course, my phone. I was given an orange jumpsuit and ankle socks. My picture was taken – "a mugshot." My worst fear had come to pass: I was in jail for murder. I sat down on a filthy cot anchored to a dirty, graffitied wall. Tears fell from my eyes. I couldn't believe what was happening.

One of the other women said, "Cheer up, doll, a looker like you can sweet talk someone and get out of here."

I moved to a corner and cried harder. I felt small and vulnerable. I was frightened. Where was the vengeful, angry woman I thought I had become?

A short while later, a guard appeared and asked for "Mrs. Candiss." I stood up.

"Come with me," she said.

She led me to a beige interrogation room with grey metal doors. George and his Attorney, Bill Becker, were waiting at a black metal desk. Bottled water was at each seat. George caught me as I fell into his arms. He held me tightly.

"Carly, we'll have you out of here in less than an hour."

I was trembling. "What is going on, George?" I asked.

Bill Becker read from my case file, "You are accused of first-degree murder for killing Roger Stiles," he said.

"It appears your handgun was found at the scene with other evidence pointing to premeditation."

Through the tears, I managed to say, "I don't own a gun, Mr. Becker."

Trembling, I turned to George and said, "I don't own a gun."

Bail was originally denied, but Bill Becker introduced the claim that "To her knowledge, Mrs. Candiss has never owned a gun."

A hefty bail was set which George paid. I was released on my own recognizance. The arraignment would be in the morning. When we walked into the lobby of the police station, Morty and Renee were waiting.

Morty shouted, "Thank God!"

It was an unusual demonstration of emotion. Renee, who was righteously inebriated, said, "Ditto that, Doctor, ditto that."

We all embraced and walked outside, where Marc waited behind the wheel of the limo. I took a deep breath of fresh air. I caught Morty's gaze. I wished he could hold me. On the ride home, George dealt bravely with Renee, who insisted on singing show tunes she sang in college.

Once we reached the Estate, George and Marc helped Renee upstairs and handed her off to Gwen. Dr. Mortimer asked Shelby for chamomile tea and escorted me to my suite. We embraced, and Morty kissed me deeply, "Darling, I was so worried."

"Oh, Morty, my worst fear was realized when I found myself in jail for murder. I thought it was the universe's cruelest joke and my just punishment."

He took my hand – "This is a huge mistake," he said. "They'll get to the bottom of it."

Shelby entered the room with a tray of hot tea. She was kind and caring, "Will there be anything else?" She asked, "I put some biscuits there, as well."

"Thank you," we said. "That will be all, Shelby, goodnight."

I drank the tea, and Morty told me what he knew.

"Apparently, Roger was found dead behind the race track where he delivered a truckload of hay and straw. He was shot twice, once in the head and once in the chest, at close range. Two guns were found at the scene. One was a 44, registered to Michael, and one was a 38, registered to you."

I asked, "How could that be? I never owned a gun in my life."

"I don't know," Morty said. "The FBI has been called in since there were two murders in as many days here in Merit. The police are assisting in the investigation. Hector is part of that team. He promised to keep me apprised."

"Two murders?" I asked. "Who else was killed?"

"Fran," he said.

Chapter Thirteen

I was aghast, and my mouth was agape.

"What are you saying, Morty? Fran is dead? What . . . How . . . why didn't you tell me?"

"I'm sorry, darling, with all the excitement, I didn't have the chance till now." He could see my sadness, "I'm sorry, that wasn't the best way for you to find out. I wasn't thinking."

"I thought she was doing well," I said.

"She was, but she had several serious injuries. Dr. Barnes at Memorial called and informed me just before George called and said you were in jail. Dr. Barnes said Fran developed a pulmonary embolism. I'm sorry, darling. The investigation found that her injuries were the result of an intentional hit-and-run. Her death is being considered a homicide."

Tears fell down my cheeks, and Morty wiped them with the tea napkin. I was stunned.

"What happens now?" I asked.

"Well, according to George, you will be arraigned in the morning. Bill Becker is your attorney and will plea not guilty. A court date will be set. There is an ongoing investigation, and the real murderers will be found. This will be behind us soon, I promise," he said.

"It has just begun for Judy," I said.

"What will become of her, two people in her life, Morty . . ." He put his arms around me and said, "We'll help her, darling." He put his coat on and walked to the window. He saw George's man standing below. "Your bodyguard is outside." I breathed a sigh of relief.

"I'm glad," I said, "I'm really glad."

After Morty left I closed the curtains to the terrace and checked the doors. I was shaken. I went into the bathroom and got ready for bed. I walked to the closet and there on the floor were two boxes, left open. I looked at them but did not touch them. They were boxes for handguns, and they were empty. I began to tremble. I called Shelby and asked her to get Mr. Candiss right away. Shelby and George came upstairs with Maxine, who had her phone and tablet in hand. I showed them the boxes.

"George, do you know where these came from?"

He said, "No," and looked at Shelby.

She said, "I don't know, sir." Maxine took pictures.

"Call the police," George said, "and nobody touches those boxes,"

I called Dr. Mortimer. I needed something to calm down. I felt hysteria coming my way at a full run!

George began to question Shelby and Maxine. He went to the window and motioned for his man to come upstairs. He called Dalton and asked him to bring today's videos of the grounds to his office. Dr. Mortimer appeared. For the first time, he was unnerved. He provided me with two sleeping pills from his bag.

He said, "These will help you sleep."

Shelby got me a glass of water. She said, "Ma'am, I haven't been in your closet today, and I've never seen those boxes before."

I believed her; the question was: Who had? George's man downstairs had not seen anyone go in my room. He was, however, out following me most of the day. He contacted George when he saw the police at Judy's, and he followed the police car to the jail.

George introduced me, "Mr. Hines, this is Carly, my daughter-in-law."

"Hello," I said.

He shook my hand and said, "Hello, Mrs. Candiss."

He was introduced to Dr. Mortimer, and they shook hands, "Yes," said Mr. Hines, "the good doctor."

The police arrived with a team. A detective named John Barnes questioned me. George called Bill Becker and informed him of current events. He advised me not to answer any questions until he was present. He said that the police could question me, further tomorrow after the arraignment. Detective Barnes questioned everyone in the house except Renee, who was sleeping it off. He went to both guard shacks and questioned the guards. His team took the boxes, which had been photographed and dusted for prints. All the commotion died down, and with the help of sleeping pills, I fell into bed.

The arraignment was at the County Courthouse. George and Bill walked up the steps on either side of me while the press shouted questions. Uniformed police officers kept a perimeter around us from behind. Mr. Hines walked ahead of us and cleared the microphones in the reporter's hands that were too close to our faces. It was melee! Once inside Courtroom H, there was silence. Judy stepped up to the railing behind our table at the front of the room. She looked terrible.

"Oh Carly, do you know about Fran?" she asked.

I nodded and wiped tears from her face. "I'm so, so sorry, Judy."

As we hugged, I saw Morty enter the courtroom. Judy asked, "Can we get together after this?"

"Yes, wait for me," I said, "I'll get you home."

Judy took her seat as the bailiff called for order. I looked at Morty, who was looking at me.

The Judge entered the Chambers.

"All rise," said the Bailiff. George Candiss was directly behind the defendant's table. He touched my shoulder and whispered, "Don't worry, Dear." The Bailiff announced the first case on the docket and the name of the judge, "Merit County vs. Carly T. Candiss. The Honorable Richard James Barton, presiding."

Bill glanced at me. "He's an old friend," he said. "We got lucky."

The Bailiff called out the charges, "The defendant is charged with murder in the first degree for the death of Roger Stiles."

I couldn't believe what was happening. I felt weak, and my knees buckled. Bill and George steadied me. The State Prosecutor and Bill were introduced to the court.

The judge said, "These are serious charges, Counselor, how do you plea?"

Bill replied, "Not guilty, your Honor. Mrs. Candiss has never owned a gun. We have witnesses that can testify to her whereabouts and full confidence this case will not go to trial, but rather be solved through investigation."

The judge asked, "Mrs. Candiss, do you understand the charges?"

"Yes, your Honor."

"And are you in agreement with your counsel?"

"Yes, your Honor."

"Very well," he said.

"I hope you are right, counselor. The date for this trial is set for one month from today. Is that satisfactory?"

Bill said, "Yes."

The judge asked the lawyer representing the State, "Acceptable, sir?"

"The State has no issue with the date, your Honor."

"Very well then," the Judge said, "Trial will be one month from today. Mrs. Candiss is remanded to county jail, till that time."

"Your Honor," Bill stated loudly before the judge could gavel out of the arraignment. "The defense would like to request that Mrs. Candiss be released until trial. There is no evidence other than circumstantial. She has no priors. Her family paid a hefty bail. She is not a flight risk. Mrs. Candiss has recently suffered the loss of her own husband and is bereft."

The Judge looked to the state prosecutor, "We find that acceptable, your Honor, provided her ability to travel is restricted." The Judge said, "Mrs. Candiss, you cannot leave this state or the county. You are advised not to speak about this case to anyone outside of your counsel. Do you understand?"

"Yes. Your Honor."

"Counsel, you will secure your client's passport?"

"Yes, sir," The Judge's gavel struck the bench, and we were adjourned. I breathed for the first time since he mentioned "Jail."

Bill Becker shook George's hand, and George thanked Bill profusely. Bill touched my shoulder, "Ok, dear, for now, we have a reprieve."

George hugged me, "Thank goodness, Carly – no jail."

Morty appeared from the back and shook George's hand, "Good News," he said. "Congratulations." I looked through the crowd for Judy.

"Dr Mortimer, did you see Judy?"

"Yes," he said. "She's right over there."

He pointed to the opposite side of the courtroom, toward the back. Judy was standing between two uniformed police officers and a man in a black

Jacket with white letters, "FBI." She had her hand up to her mouth and tears in her eyes. I walked across the courtroom. The FBI agent saw me approach and advised Judy not to speak to me.

I heard him say, "If you'll come with me, Ma'am." He took her arm and led her from the courtroom. She did not look back.

Chapter Fourteen

George and Dr. Mortimer joined me as I watched Judy leave.

"What was that about?" Morty asked.

"I don't know," I said.

George walked up behind us, "How about we stop by the Waymark for lunch -- My treat?"

We agreed, and I was suddenly starving. Oscar was on duty at the restaurant.

"Oh my goodness," he said, "If it isn't my favorite family – and the best doctor in town."

Oscar winked at Morty. George asked, "Is our table available, Oscar?"

"Of course, sir – always."

Oscar led us to the table and took our drink orders. We were all going to indulge in a little taste this day.

George said, "All right with you two if I ask Mr. Hines to join us? He is, after all, watching from a close distance."

Dr. Mortimer and I reluctantly agreed, and George dialed Mr. Hines and invited him for lunch.

Oscar returned with a glass of red for me, a dry martini for George, and a whiskey on ice for Dr. Mortimer. Mr. Hines appeared and declined a drink.

He said, "I'll have water. I'm on the clock."

I found Mr. Hines intriguing. He seemed like anything but a private investigator. He was mild-mannered, polite, and interesting. His conversation was casual, and he was well-spoken. Our lunch was enjoyable since we were ordered not to talk about the case or trial – we avoided that topic. Instead, we talked about opening day at the races and George's hopefuls. George told Mr. Hines and Dr. Mortimer that I had a gelding who looked promising, as well.

Mr. Hines said, "You are quite the horsewoman yourself, Mrs. Candiss; You ride very well."

I felt myself flush, "Thank you, Mr. Hines," I said.

George confirmed Mr. Hines' observation, "Yes. Michael said, 'Carly knew her way around horses.' He said that it was one of her many endearing qualities."

I was surprised that Michael said anything positive about me, to anyone. Mr. Hines turned to Dr. Mortimer, "What about you, sir? Do you ride?"

Morty said, "No, I prefer my convertible." Morty and I knew now, that Mr. Hines saw us together at the guest house. We avoided eye contact for the remainder of the meal. George paid the bill, and he and Mr. Hines excused themselves to conduct, business.

"Dr. Mortimer, will you see Carly back to the Estate?" George asked.

"I sure will, George, with pleasure."

Morty and I took the long way back to the estate. We discussed the arraignment and possible trial and Roger and Fran's deaths.

"Who could be framing me, and why?" I asked.

Morty encouraged me to stay calm, "You are innocent, Carly. You have nothing to worry about."

"But someone is trying to implicate me," I said.

"And what about Mr. Hines? He saw us, Morty."

"I don't think he is here to observe or judge your personal life, Carly," Morty said.

"I think he is here to keep you safe. Perhaps Mr. Hines is concerned for your safety and nothing more; discretion is part of the job."

"I hope so. What if he tells George?" I asked.

"We deal with it," Morty said. "Carly, it's ok to love each other. Remember, the whole town knows about Michael's infidelity and abuse."

Yes, I thought, but they don't know we killed him.

Morty dropped me at the house. It was unusually quiet. I called out, "Anyone home?"

Shelby appeared at the top of the stairs. "Hello, ma'am."

"Where is everybody?" I asked.

"Down at the barn," she replied.

"Is everything all right?" I asked.

"Yes, ma'am they just wanted to see the foal and the new stud arrived this morning."

"That's right," I said.

With everything that happened over the past several weeks, I had forgotten about the stud. Prior to his death, Michael and George went to the Auction in Dallas and purchased a king. He was a thoroughbred stallion named "Lucky Jack." His bloodline was as impressive as his two offspring, who were Triple Crown winners.

"Oh, I must go down and see him." I caught a glimpse of Mr. Hines outside the study doors.

I went out back. "Mr. Hines, I am walking to the barn. We may as well walk together, yes?"

He agreed, and we took the walking path toward the barn.

"It is a beautiful day," he said. "This is my favorite time of year."

"Oh, really," I inquired, "why?"

"Well," he said, "it's cooling down, but not too cold. The humidity is less. The mosquitos have died or gone to a warmer climate, and the racing season is about to begin."

"Are you a gambling man?" I asked.

"No, ma'am," he said. "I run security at the race track in Merit."

"Is that where you met George?" I asked.

"Yes," he said, "and Michael." I was taken aback.

"You knew my husband?"

"Yes, ma'am, very well. Like I said, I run security at Merit Downs. One could hardly know the track and not know Michael."

"I suppose so," I said. We walked the rest of the way in silence. I wondered why I could not place him.

The loud chatter at the barn was refreshing. It was a stark difference from the County Courthouse. Renee was pouring lemonade into plastic cups as they were passed out by Gwen. Dalton was handing out cigars, and George was sitting on the corral fence, smoking a cigar. Maxine was standing behind

George, talking on the phone. Raul had the stallion on a lunge line, and his hooves thundered as he galloped around the pen. The stable hands and two jockeys were watching the horse's gait.

Raul said, "His gait is nicer than his demeanor."

George said, "Yes. They said he was somewhat of a badass."

The horse was a specimen. He was strong and muscled out; his coat glistened. At sixteen hands, he had a girth and confirmation that was athletic and impressive. His mane and tail were jet black against his blood-bay body. He was beautiful.

Maxine hung up the phone and announced, "The press will be here in 30 minutes."

George was eager to show off his king. I watched Mr. Hines, watch Raul.

When the press arrived, I walked back to the house with Renee. She was reinforced by the vodka in her lemonade. Gwen and Dalton were a distance behind us, and behind them was Mr. Hines.

Renee said, "Oh, Carly, I miss Michael. I am afraid I am the only person who really understood him."

"I know, Renee," I said. I saw sadness suddenly overcome her. Renee loved her son. She referred to Michael as "My Boy" as long as I had known her. She overlooked his flaws.

"He would have been proud today. He was thrilled when he and George were able to land that stud at auction. Of course, that stud is half yours, too," she said.

"Ok. I'll take the front half," I quipped, "and you can keep the horse's ass."

Renee laughed out loud and turned to see that her entourage was close by. She saw Mr. Hines, "Your bodyguard is following us."

She asked, "Does it bother you, dear?"

"No. With everything that has happened, I feel safer knowing someone is watching," I said. "George invited Mr. Hines to lunch today after the arraignment. He's quite nice. Did you know he knew Michael?" I asked.

"Oh yes, dear," she said. "He was Michael's bodyguard, too." I swallowed hard and questioned my own naivete.

"How was the arraignment, dear?" Renee asked.

"Frightening," I said. "And poor, sweet Judy." I saw Renee cringe.

"Yes, and poor Roger," Renee said sympathetically. "I wonder how Judy will pay off Roger's gambling debt?" she queried.

"What?" I was surprised.

"Oh yes, dear, Roger was deep in the bookies' pockets at Merit. He asked Michael for the money to pay them off. In return, he would 'discount' our hay, straw, and feed until the debt was paid. I thought it was a good proposition, but Michael turned him down."

"Why?" I asked.

Renee waved her hand in the air and said, "You know, Michael, dear. He was hard-pressed to help anyone. He harbored such anger."

Renee's honesty surprised me. I thought she was unaware . . .

Chapter Fifteen

When we arrived at the house, Shelby said, "Mrs. Candiss, your phone has been ringing."

"Okay," I said and climbed the stairs to retrieve my phone. There were multiple calls from Judy. I checked for messages. There was only one.

"Carly, call me," she said. "I spoke with the FBI today, and they said that Roger's murder and Fran's murder are connected and possibly perpetrated by the same person and or people. I told them you were with me when Fran was hit. You are still considered a person of interest. Please tell me you are not my husband's murderer. Oh, Carly, I know it isn't you. My parents are on their way to Merit. They'll be here later today. Call me, please." Her voice trailed off, and the line went dead. What evidence could the FBI possibly have? I called Judy. There was no answer.

After a long bath, I put on my bedclothes. I opened the doors to the terrace and let the fresh, fall air fill the room. The sun was setting, and Shelby left a snack tray with fruit, cheeses, and crackers. It was perfect and all I needed after such a big lunch and a busy day. The phone rang. It was Judy. She was with her mom at Pete's. They were sharing a banana split, hoping for a momentary reprieve from profound grief. Her dad was at the morgue helping with arrangements and exploring what came next. The law required an autopsy, and Judy's dad was inquiring into logistics. She apologized for not answering earlier but said she spent the day crying. She was soothed by the presence of her mom and dad. She asked if we could talk tomorrow. I agreed to call her in the morning.

I closed the terrace doors and drew the curtains. Shelby had turned down the bed. I picked up a book on the nightstand and began to read. There was a knock at the door.

"Come in." George stepped through and jabbered excitedly, "Isn't he magnificent, Carly? Michael was right. This stud will take us a long way. We will be a household name to owners, trainers, and jockeys. With Dr. Mortimer's mare and this stud, we may own future Triple Crown winners!" George was delighted.

"He is the most beautiful horse I have seen, George," I said. "I am happy for you."

He started to walk into my room but thought better of it. He stopped and took a few steps back.

"Happy for us, dear. Good night," he said.

"Good night, George," I said. It was then I realized that my being watched was key to George's exemplary behavior.

I tried to sleep but could not. The arraignment went through my mind. I was curious about what I learned about Mr. Hines and his presence outside my room now. I thought about Morty and my feelings for him. I thought about my uneasiness toward Raul and the way Mr. Hines watched Raul today. I remembered that Raul and Roger must be well known to Mr. Hines since his life is largely tied up in Merit Downs. I must talk to Jonah. He would know about Mr. Hines. I was sure that Jonah would be on the Estate in the next couple of days to provide a "Bill of Health" for our new family member, "Lucky Jack." I would ask Jonah's opinion.

Roger and Fran came to mind. What did they have in common? Who could have killed them, and why? Did their deaths have anything to do with me . . . or Michael? How did a gun registered in my name get to the crime scene and their boxes in my closet? Who was setting me up and why? I thought of my good friend, Judy. How was she going to get through this? I remembered her hatred for Michael. I wondered how the investigation was going? I must ask Morty what he found out from Hector. My mind was in a spin cycle, and it was exhausting.

Chapter Sixteen

Opening day finally arrived, and the Estate was a buzz. Renee was tending to final arrangements for the reception. Gwen was taking care of last-minute needs and decoration issues. Emily was overseeing the Kitchen. Shelby was supervising the cleaning crew downstairs in the den, study, library, and dining room. The caterers were setting up stations for drinks and hor'd'vours. Dalton was roping off the upstairs quarters with signs about the whereabouts of downstairs restrooms. Maxine was on the phone taking bets for George's attorneys and bankers. Jim would place their bets. Raul was overseeing the loading of the trailers and transportation of the horses. George was in his office on the phone. He had three hopeful winners for the day, one of which was mine. I was in the dining room, folding napkins and watching the organized chaos around me. There was excitement in the air, but Michael's absence was palpable.

I saw Jonah in the foyer, just inside the front door. He had flowers, as usual, for Renee. I greeted him. He took my hand, embraced me, and kissed my cheek.

"It's so nice to see you, Carly." I was touched by his sincerity.

Renee entered the foyer, "Jonah, it's nice of you to come," she said. "You are one of my lucky charms. Michael would have been upset if you did not bring flowers, today."

"I wouldn't think of it, Renee," he answered. She took the flowers. "Let me give these to Emily. You will be here for the reception, of course."

As Renee walked away, I asked Jonah if he would walk with me.

"I'd be delighted," he said.

Outside on the grounds, Jonah marveled at the activity.

"Busy place," he said.

"Always on opening day," I responded.

"Jonah, can I ask you something?"

"Anything, Carly."

"What can you tell me about Mr. Hines?"

"Well . . . he is a professional. He is good at his job. He has a lot of experience and is well-qualified," Jonah said.

"How so?" I asked. "He served two tours in Afghanistan, worked for the Secret Service, and was attached to the FBI in Merit for several years. He is well-connected, Carly. Why do you ask?"

"George hired Mr. Hines to watch out for me," I answered.

"It's funny, Carly, but Mr. Hines asked me about you, as well. He approached me at the track yesterday during physicals and asked for a word. He was particularly interested in your relationship with Michael."

"What did you tell him, Jonah?"

"I told him the truth – that you were too good for Michael, and he was a lucky man to have you. Michael's cruelty and indiscretions are no secret to Mr. Hines."

George slapped Jonah on the back.

"Good to see you, young man," he said. "What do you think of my stud?"

"He is everything Michael said he was; he is magnificent, George," Jonah said.

"You know, Carly and I stand to make a great deal of money off that king," George boasted.

"Then I'd better do all I can to keep him healthy," Jonah joked.

"Ride with me to the track. Marc is driving me and Maxine over now; Dalton will bring Renee and Carly later. We can re-negotiate your retainer. I want to pay you sufficiently for your availability and expertise."

"Of course," Jonah agreed.

He bid me farewell till post-time. As I watched George and Jonah walk away, I reflected on my fondness for Jonah. He was an accomplished veterinarian and a nice man. How he and Michael became friends was a mystery.

Renee appeared in the doorway. "Carly dear, we must get dressed. We are running out of time."

I rushed into the house and ducked under the ropes. I called to Renee, "I'll meet you at the car in an hour."

Shelby helped me dress, and Gwen helped Renee. Shelby was quite good with make-up, and thanks to Judy's talent for style, my hair was gorgeous. The black trim Celia added was just right for the dress.

Shelby gasped, "You are beautiful, Ma'am," she said.

I looked in the mirror, "I AM beautiful!" I said, weeping, "I AM beautiful!" I had not felt beautiful in a very long time.

I met Renee at the car. Dalton looked especially handsome in his tux. Renee was exquisite – her gown and hat were perfect. She was aglow and perhaps slightly drunk from Champagne. She winked at Dalton and asked, "Did you bring our Champagne?"

"It's on ice, ma'am," he said.

"You deserve a raise," Renee shouted.

She poured three champagnes in trophy goblets and we set out to the races. I felt a twinge of sadness. Eleven years of opening days with Renee, and this would be our first without Michael. My pain and sadness were for her. She was bereft. She loved Michael unconditionally. My love for Michael disappeared through the years and faded away with the bruises.

The race track was alive with patrons. Parking attendants watched over general and preferred parking. Give-away booths, morning line reporters, and raffle ticket sales filled the main-floor lobby. Snack bars were stocked. Kegs were full. Waitresses and beverage carts made their way outside. Popcorn machines filled the air with the smell of freshly popped popcorn. Hot dog stands were open for business. Shoe-shine stands were available on every floor. The bleachers were filling up and the game room was loud with teens, not interested in horses. Would-be winners were standing at tall tables looking at monitors and reviewing morning-line odds. Racing forms were plentiful, and seasoned gamblers studied their chances as they made their way to the clubhouse. The posted track conditions were "fast and dry."

As we entered our box, Dr. Mortimer approached. He was wearing a grey suit and maroon tie. His fedora was grey. He had on black Aviator, wing-tip shoes, and a big, bright smile. He helped Renee into the box. "Ma'am," he said.

She slightly curtsied and took his hand. "Hello, Doctor," she said.

Morty took my hand. "Ravishing," he whispered.

I smiled, "Hello, Doctor."

Marlene greeted us with hugs and condolences. Renee's tears finally found their way to the surface. She had been holding them back all day. It was Marlene's friendly, familiar face and this racetrack that brought Renee closest to her son and the loss of him. They spent a lot of time here.

Marlene said, "What will you have today, Mrs. Candiss?"

"I'll start with Champagne."

Marlene looked at me and Dr. Mortimer. He said, "I'll have whiskey on the rocks."

I said, "Wine, please, Marlene. Red, of course."

She smiled, "Of course, ma'am."

Hector stopped by, "Any tips for today?" he asked.

Morty shook Hector's hand and said, "Bet on all of George's, especially the gelding."

Hector nodded and left to place his bets. Jonah and George walked into the box. Dr. Mortimer shook their hands.

"We meet again," Morty said.

Jonah looked at me, "You are a vision, Carly," he said.

"Yes, she is," George agreed. "And you too, my love," he said to Renee and kissed her hand.

We took our seats. George had his binoculars and was watching the horses as they were ponied onto the track. The first race was six furlongs for non-winners. He did not have a horse in the race but was interested in one that he contemplated claiming. Morty had his binoculars and was watching, as well, but he was watching Raul, on horseback as he ponied out the number two horse for Mitch Malcolm – a stable owner and family friend.

Jonah said, "What a beautiful day; it's really perfect."

"Michael would love it," Renee replied. "Hardly seems possible that he's not here."

I looked at George, Morty, and Jonah. I said to Renee, "Thank goodness for these strong and wonderful men who surround us."

Renee said, "I'll drink to that."

The announcer asked that we all rise for the National Anthem. The trumpeter brought the races to a start with the familiar "Call to the Post." A moment of silence was asked for to remember Michael Candiss: "Mr Racetrack." All eyes were on me and Renee. I felt incredibly uncomfortable. A tear fell softly down my face as I remembered my first day at the races eleven years ago. I was much younger and in love. I held my breath for a moment and then gasped at my own naivete. George saw Mr. Hines on the main floor and motioned for him to join us.

Chapter Seventeen

George's maiden claiming race was a bust. He decided not to claim the mare since she broke down before the quarter pole. The second race was a quarter-mile for three-year-olds and up who had never won a race. George liked a Gelding called "Pretty Boy." He was in the five spot and going off at four to one. He encouraged Morty and Jonah to place their bets on number five. Morty liked Pretty Boy and he liked the three-horse, "Mister Big," who was also not a favorite but going off at eleven to one. Morty bet a quinella on the 3-5 and an exacta box on the 3-5. He also bet $2 across on the 3. Jonah did not bet. Hector came by again, and George advised him to try his luck with the five. As Hector left to place his bet, he did something unusual. He grabbed Dr. Mortimer's hand and shook it wildly and hard.

Hector said, "I want some of your luck, man!"

Morty looked at me and blushed.

The remainder of the day was predictable: George's horses won both races, and our gelding won best in class. George claimed two horses that would move down in class for Raul to train. Hector won more than he lost. Jonah never bet. Renee was moderately intoxicated. I did well, winning $300.00 for the day, and my gelding would be a good, strong horse in his class for now. Morty bet too much on long shots but came out a little better off. Mr. Hines made me feel uncomfortable. He observed quietly and spent a good amount of time supervising, by radio, various security personnel stationed around the track. I wondered why I did not remember Mr. Hines from previous racing years. Then I had an "A-HA" moment. Mr. Hines used to be heavier and had a beard. Roger called him "Wimpy." Suddenly, I remembered. I was able to place him in previous years at the track. A light came on. I would talk to Judy about Mr. Hines. As I recall he had a story to tell that included Roger.

The reception at the Estate started with the Mayor thanking the Candiss family for hosting the event. The Mayor thanked City Planners for upgrading the racetrack and the roadways leading therein. He saluted the hard-working and now deceased "Son of Merit," who brought racing to the county and tripled the town's annual revenue. He announced that the Gardens in the center of the track would be known as the "Michael Candiss Memorial Gardens," with gratitude for Michael's contributions to the welfare of the county, the town, and the racetrack. The Mayor acknowledged the family's loss and the community's loss in leadership.

Finally, the Mayor said, "Let's get this party started."

Renee, who was well on her way to a respectful alcoholic black-out, gulped her drink and said, "OH, thank God!"

The waiters assembled in the dining room, and Emily called out, "Dinner is served."

The guests took their seats. Morty, whose seating placard was next to me, was not present. I immediately looked for Raul, who was also missing.

Jonah approached and asked, "Mind if I sit here, Carly?"

"Of course not, Jonah," I said.

The first course was served – a carrot soup with heavy cream, parsley garnish, and croutons.

"Delicious," Jonah said, and I agreed.

The salad came out of the kitchen as the soup bowls were cleared. It was a date salad with cucumber, radishes, corn, and chickpeas from our gardens. Fine sprigs of dill lay across the top and sweet cilantro with cracked peppercorns were added for taste and color.

"Another excellent dish," Jonah remarked as I searched the room for Morty. They cleared the salad plates, and the main courses of lamb, pork, and steak came to the table.

Jonah said, "He's with Raul, Carly. It's an annual tradition - the only day of the year they are guaranteed privacy, because everyone else is here."

My eyes fell. "Does everyone know?" I asked.

Jonah nodded and squeezed my hand. I asked for a whiskey. Why did I feel like my world was falling apart . . . again?

Chapter Eighteen

I awoke the next morning with a pounding headache and what I believed to be a hangover. I'd never had a hangover. I was groggy and somewhat nauseated. I rang for Shelby.

"Good morning, Mrs. Candiss," she said when she came into the room. I noticed she'd had a haircut.

"Your hair looks nice, Shelby."

"Thank you. Judy does a nice job."

"You saw Judy?" I asked.

"Yes, ma'am, yesterday. She gave me an appointment while you were all at the track. When else could I get there?"

I was surprised Judy was at work. "How long have you gone to Judy?" I asked.

"It's been years. All of us on the Estate see Judy except Renee. Judy is the best in town and the gossip there is better than any other salon. Do you want breakfast, Mrs. Candiss?"

"Shelby, do you think you could call me Carly?" I groused. She was surprised.

"Yes, ma'am, if that's what you prefer."

"It is," I said. "And no breakfast – but I would like two aspirin and a cup of coffee."

"Right away, Mrs. Candiss."

She corrected herself, "Carly."

When Shelby left the room, I called Judy. She picked up on the first ring. She sounded tired. She spent the night crying and kept her mom up late. She said, "We worked yesterday because customers called for appointments, and we thought we'd feel better if we were busy."

"Besides, I need money now, Carly."

"Judy," I said, "I will give you money. Don't worry about money, my friend. Have you heard anything about Roger's death? Have they done the autopsy?"

"The FBI came to the house and took his computer, and his tablet," she said. "They asked me for his passwords and were surprised I didn't know. I asked what they were looking for and was told they don't know, yet, but they will know when they find it. What does that even mean, Carly?"

"I don't know," I said.

"Do you and your mom want to meet for lunch, my treat, at the Waymark?" I asked.

"I can't, Carly. The FBI warned me not to see or talk to you. I could be considered an accessory if you're indicted. I have to go. I'm sorry."

I stopped her, "Wait, Judy, I need to ask you about Mr. Hines?"

Judy said, "Rick? What about him?"

"Rick, yes Rick" – I remembered. "What do we know about him?"

Judy replied, "He and Roger were close, Carly. They served two tours together in Afghanistan. They bowled together when we lived in Cater. He has called me several times to check on me. He is helping with the investigation. He has a history with the FBI and the Secret Service. He shared something with me yesterday that I didn't know. He said that Roger had gambling debt. Carly, I had no idea." She said, "I really have to go. Talk to Rick if you need to. He can be trusted." The line went dead.

My headache was worse. Shelby returned while I was on the phone. She brought up coffee, a glass of water, and two aspirin. I swallowed the aspirin and started on the coffee right away. I called to the guard shack, "Ralph, is Dr. Mortimer's car on the grounds?"

"No, ma'am," he said.

"Have you been on duty all night?" I continued to question him.

"Yes, ma'am," he said.

"Was his car here earlier?" I asked, realizing he was not going to offer information unless I inquired.

"Yes, ma'am, Dr Mortimer left the Estate early this morning."

"Thank you, Ralph. Have a wonderful day."

"You too, ma'am," he said.

Renee appeared holding a grey, plaid ice pack with a silver lid against her forehead. She looked my way and handed it to me.

"Oh dear, you look worse than I feel," she said.

She was drinking a mimosa and offered it to me.

"Please, God, no," I said. "I have had enough to drink for this year."

"Oh dear, you will have to learn about the 'Hair of the dog,'" she said.

She rang for Shelby and asked her to bring up two Mimosas.

By 10:00 a.m., Renee and I had touched up each other's nails and solved each other's problems. We finished a half dozen mimosas each and were feeling up for a walk. Renee asked if I wanted to walk to the barn and see the foal and the stud. I agreed, and we set out in our robes. As we reached the barn, I saw Raul. He watched us coming, and I'm sure he could tell we were tipsy.

"There's the stud, Renee," I said.

"Did you want to see the horse too?"

Raul turned on his heels and left the barn. Renee and I laughed out loud as we gazed at our four-legged example of extraordinary horseflesh.

Dr. Mortimer drove up in his red convertible. Renee greeted him with a kiss on the cheek and reprimanded him for missing a lovely event last evening. I remained focused on the horses. He called out to me and I ignored him.

"Carly," he said as he approached, "Did you forget your appointment today with the neurologist?"

Without turning around, I said, "I guess I did, Dr. Mortimer. Do you think I can go in my robe?"

He realized I was slightly drunk.

"I'll call and reschedule," he said.

"A good idea, Doctor," I said as I walked out of the barn.

Renee and I walked arm in arm back toward the house, leaving Dr. Mortimer to watch us walk away. I knew Raul was close by. I would leave them to one another. What have I done? A feeling of foreboding crept over me.

"You seemed to be enjoying yourself with Jonah last night, dear," Renee said.

"He is a delightful man," I said, "and extraordinarily kind."

"Yes," Renee responded. "You two looked cozy on the dance floor," she said, with a hint of sadness.

"Did I dance with Jonah?" I asked.

"Yes, dear, after dinner and several whiskeys, I think you danced with everyone, including me."

"Oh, Renee, was I ridiculous? I don't remember a thing," I said.

"No, dear, you were fine – just happier than I've ever seen you. I think Jonah will be calling. You were quite affectionate with him."

"Oh no," I sighed. "I'm so sorry, Renee. That's a horrible thing to do at your reception and after the loss of your son."

"Don't fret over trifles, Carly. Never fret over trifles. I know my son did all he could to prevent your happiness. I am not blind. The funny thing is, he cared for you. I think that will be evident when we read the will tomorrow."

"What?" I asked.

"Don't you remember, dear? Bill Becker is coming tomorrow afternoon for the reading. You asked him last night to meet here rather than his office."

"Oh my . . ."

Back at the house, I wondered if my black-out was from excessive drinking or if it had happened again. I was sorry I missed the appointment with the neurologist. I dialed Dr. Mortimer, who did not pick up.

I left a message, "Dr. Mortimer, please reschedule the appointment with Dr. Nadal as soon as possible. I seem to have had another memory lapse, although this one may have been the result of excessive drinking and another broken heart. Just let me know when it is, and I'll see myself there. I hope you and Raul enjoyed your annual rendezvous. I would not want to interfere with a time-honored ritual. By the way, Michael's will is going to be read tomorrow afternoon."

As I was hanging up, my phone began buzzing with an incoming call. It was Jonah. I let it go to message and fell into bed. The mimosas and the day caught up with me.

I woke at 3:00 pm, still in my robe and with a brand new headache. I turned on the shower and tried to focus my eyes. I rang for Shelby, who came up and tried to hold back a smile.

"What's funny?" I asked.

She laughed and said, "Oh, Carly, Renee told us what you said to Raul, and none of us have been able to stop laughing." I laughed, too.

"It's amazing the courage six mimosas will give you. Maybe I should drink more often."

"Yes, maybe you should. Dr Silvers is downstairs, Carly."

"Jonah? He is?" I asked.

"Yes, ma'am. He said you invited him to go riding."

"Oh, brother," I said.

"Tell him I'll be down soon, please. And will you call Raul and ask him to saddle my Bay and a horse for Jonah?"

Chapter Nineteen

Jonah and I walked to the barn. He was more talkative than usual. I assumed he was nervous, as was I. He had the advantage of knowing what transpired the night before. I was oblivious. Asking him to ride was confirmation that the night went well.

"How are you feeling today?" he asked.

"I've felt better," I replied.

"I bet," he said, grinning. "I've never seen you drink whiskey."

"I never have," I said. "I guess there is a first time for everything."

Jonah laughed and said, "I suppose there is . . . like a first kiss."

Now, I vaguely remembered that -- and without disdain. When we reached the barn, my bay, and a sorrel were saddled and tied to the hitching post outside. A stable hand was close by and greeted us warmly.

"Good afternoon, Mrs. Candiss; hello, Dr. Silvers."

"Hello, Jim," I said.

Jonah said, "It's a great day for a ride."

Jim agreed and gave me a leg up. Jonah mounted his sorrel, and Jim said, "He's got a sensitive head, Doctor, be gentle with reining."

"Thanks, Jim, I will."

We kept our horses at a slow walk out of the main Estate area and headed toward the North End. Jonah was intelligent and interesting. He was easy to be with, not to mention easy on the eyes. He was a good friend to my late husband. Michael had few friends but more than he deserved.

"Jonah, how was it that you and Michael were such good friends?" I asked.

"Oh," he said, "it's complicated, Carly. Michael had a good eye for a horse. He had an innate intuition about them. He knew when they were sound. That served him well and helped me out."

"He WAS a horse-whisperer," I said.

"But there is more, Carly -- and if you don't mind -- I'd like to tell you."

"Sure, go on."

Jonah looked straight ahead, "I wanted to see you. Being Michael's friend afforded me that luxury, even if it was mostly during racing season. I know it sounds twisted," he said, "my friendship with Michael allowed you and I to spend time together, Carly, without pretense or pressure."

I didn't know what to say.

We dismounted and walked our horses slowly through the North End, and I showed Jonah our gardens. We ate a couple of delicious tomatoes off the vine. We kicked through the gold and red leaves lying on the ground. Fall was fast approaching. I broke the silence, "Jonah, I am flattered. I had no idea you felt that way. You have been a gentleman and a good friend, thank you. I want us to remain friends, but since Michael's death, like you said, things are complicated." Jonah sighed and said, "Dr. Mortimer, right?" I did not answer. I looked into his loving eyes and said, "I'm sorry, Jonah." He mounted his sorrel and I hoisted myself onto the bay. He said, "It's a beautiful day, Carly. The company is exquisite. Let's enjoy the time we have." He attempted to draw his horse next to mine and steal a kiss, but his sorrel did not like the plow rein and ducked out. Jonah ended up in the leaves. "Jim warned you," I said, laughing. "He certainly did," Jonah said with an embarrassed smile. He mounted up, and we headed back. After a moment's embrace in the barn, Jonah left the Estate through the back gate.

I was exhausted and glad the day was over. My body needed rest. I had not heard from Morty. Raul was not around when I rode into the barn, and it was getting dark as I walked toward the house. The lights were on, and the decorations were still up from the reception. The house glowed. I was surprised to see Mr. Hines walking toward me.

"Mrs. Candiss, let's take a drive," he said.

"I am so tired," I said. "I just want to go to bed."

"Trust me, you don't want to go to the house."

Mr. Hines took my arm and walked me to his car, which was parked close by.

"What is this about, Mr. Hines?" I asked.

"Trust me," he said, and we exited the same gate Jonah drove through minutes before.

As Mr. Hines raced out the gate, I heard sirens coming in through the front.

"What is it, Mr. Hines? What has happened?" I begged him to tell me.

"It's Gwen," he said. "She fell down the stairs."

I wailed, "Oh My God. Mr. Hines, I must be there for Shelby, Renee, and Dalton. Take me back," I demanded.

"Mrs. Candiss," he said flatly – "you cannot be present at the scene of another unexpected tragedy. You cannot be further implicated, don't you see? George radioed and instructed me to stop you before you got to the house."

"Where are we going?" I asked.

"Where do you want to go?"

I dialed Morty's number. I told him what happened. He suggested I come to his place.

Morty was waiting on the front steps of his condominium. Mr. Hines dropped me off and said he would come back for me later. I thanked him, and Morty and I went inside.

I was in tears, "Oh, Morty, Gwen's hurt; she fell down the stairs," I sobbed.

Morty held me as I cried. A short while later, he called the hospital a learned that Gwen had died; she was pronounced at the scene. There were no efforts to revive her at the hospital. Morty put his arms around me. He was warm and tender.

"Darling," he said, "I'm sorry. So much has happened. It is truly hard to bear."

"I need to lie down," I said.

"Of course." He walked me into his guest room. "Would you like a glass of wine?" he asked.

"Yes. I would." I couldn't believe I was going to drink again. Maybe Renee had taught me a new trick.

Morty came in with glasses of red wine. He put two pillows against the headboard and helped me sit up. He went into the bathroom and came out with a box of tissues. I took a long drink and asked, "Why, Morty?"

"I don't know," he said, "I'll have to get details from the M.E."

"I'm not talking about Gwen," I said.

Morty took in a ragged breath – "It's who I am, Carly. You must believe I love you. You know a leopard can't change its spots."

Morty took a long drink of his wine and touched my cheek. He took both glasses and put them on the nightstand. He took me in his arms, and I moved into him. He kissed me tenderly at first, then deeply. I groaned. I was hungry for his love. I felt my body surge. Morty removed my blouse; he took off his shirt and when our skin touched, electricity ran through us. I opened up to him as he lowered himself onto me.

"Shall we get undressed?" he asked.

"YES," I pleaded, "OH YES."

I woke when the phone rang. It was Mr. Hines.

"Sorry to wake you. You'd better stay there for the night. The police are treating Gwen's fall and the house as a crime scene. There is no evidence, but with Michael's sudden death, your arrest, and the other unexplained deaths in Merit, they are investigating any death that appears out of the ordinary. Just stay put until you hear from me."

"Okay," I said.

Morty rolled over and put his arm around me. He kissed my breasts and then my lips. He ran his fingertips lightly over my tummy and down my thigh. I rolled over. We gasped as he entered me without resistance. I moved with him until we were overcome with each other's desire.

Mr. Hines called just before eight a.m. I had showered and was surrendering to my caffeine addiction. Dr. Mortimer was called into the hospital for an emergency early in the morning. Mr. Hines said, "I'm coming to get you, Mrs. Candiss. Surveillance showed you with Dr. Silvers at the time of Gwen's fall. You're not under suspicion. The investigation turned up no wrongdoing. Gwen, who was wearing heels, was looking at her phone and walking downstairs. She must have misstepped and fallen. It seems that it was an unfortunate accident."

"How is Renee doing?" I asked. "She was so fond of Gwen."

Mr. Hines hesitated, "I thought George called you. Renee is in Merit Community Hospital – with uncontrolled hysteria. Dr. Mortimer is with her now." I dropped the phone.

"Poor, dear, Renee," I said to myself. What was Gwen doing upstairs?

Chapter Twenty

Mr. Hines picked me up, and we drove directly to the hospital.

"Mr. Hines, can you tell me about Roger's debt problem? I heard that he struggled with gambling debt."

Mr. Hines nodded and said, "Roger was a good friend of mine. His murder will be solved. I will see to that. We know you did not kill him. What we don't know is why, or who made the attempt to implicate you," he said. "Roger was deep in debt to two bookies who are less than honorable. Roger knew them and their reputation; he must have had a plan to pay them back. Something went wrong."

"And what about Fran?" I asked.

"We believe Fran was in some way involved. Law enforcement does not believe she was an innocent victim."

"The two murders were connected?" I asked.

"Yes," he said, "and we never had this conversation."

George was in the waiting room with Dalton, Shelby, Maxine, and Emily. He looked tired as he reassured me, "She is resting now, Carly. She was overcome with grief and inconsolable. They had to give her something to calm down."

"Can I see her?" I asked.

George shook his head, "Not now."

I looked at the tired and worried faces of the staff. They loved and appreciated Renee. Shelby was in tears. Emily and Dalton tried in vain to comfort her. Maxine was focused on George. I found myself wondering if one of them was a murderer? Then I remembered I AM. I am a murderer. I killed Renee's only son, whom she loved deeply. Was I responsible, in some way, for Gwen's loss as well? I began to weep with Shelby.

Morty appeared in the waiting room. His face was serious and concerned. He spoke directly to George.

"You may as well send the staff home, George. Renee will be here a few days."

He looked at me, "Hello, Mrs. Candiss. Renee is asking for you."

"How is she?" I asked.

Dr. Mortimer addressed the group, "She is shaken. She is emotionally vulnerable. She is having a breakdown of sorts. She needs rest and support. We are going to keep her for the next few days for complete rest. She will be medicated against the possibility of DT's. Please, for now, do not bring liquor as it may interact with medications. Let her rest and go about your daily activities. She'll need your support more once she is home."

The staff agreed and thanked the Doctor. They began gathering themselves to leave the hospital.

"Can I see her now?" I asked.

"Yes, Mrs. Candiss, but only for a few minutes."

George, Dr. Mortimer, and I went into the E.R. I glanced back at Shelby, who was sobbing and obviously overcome with sadness.

Renee reached out. I ran to her, "OH Carly, where have you been? Did you see Gwen? Did you see her? She is dead, Carly, she is gone!"

"I know, Renee, I know, I'm so sorry," I said.

"What is happening, Carly? What is happening?" she wept violently.

Dr. Mortimer instructed the Nurse to bring additional medication. George tried to console Renee. She was inconsolable and completely distraught. I kept my arms tightly wrapped around her until the Nurse returned with a syringe and injected the medication into the I.V. Renee's body relaxed. She stopped crying and she dropped back into her pillows and drifted off.

"Let's leave her alone to get some rest," Doctor Mortimer advised. I'll stay with her and keep you updated. George, will you go with the Nurse and sign some hospital privacy forms to allow information to be relayed, and to whom?"

George left the room.

Morty and I embraced. Renee was deeply asleep and comfortable. Morty pulled me close and whispered, "I love you. When can I see you again?"

I pulled away, hesitant and afraid that Renee would hear. I kissed him on the cheek and said, "Thank you, Doctor. We appreciate everything you have done. Please keep us apprised."

I ran into George at the desk. He put his arm around me and we walked out to the parking lot, where Dalton was the only staff waiting.

"Let's go home, Dalton," George said.

George called Bill Becker and informed him of Renee's status. The reading was canceled for a few days. George's next call was to Maxine. He asked her to cancel his upcoming trip to Texas.

George called Raul, who was trailering the horses, to discuss today's agenda and logistics. George then turned his attention to me.

"How are you, Dear?" he asked. I was tearful; I had grown to love Renee, and I was just beginning to know Gwen.

"I am bearing up, George. Life has become challenging, hasn't it?"

"It surely has," he said. "I can't help but think about Gwen. She was a lovely woman. She had no family, Carly, just us, on the Estate; we were her family." He sighed and said, "Renee will not be at the track for the first time in many years. Will you come, Carly? It will keep our minds off Gwen and Renee and perhaps be an entertaining distraction," he said. I agreed to meet George in our box at post time.

I went to sleep for an hour. Shelby woke me a little after eleven.

"Post time is one o'clock, ma'am," she said. "Dalton will be waiting out front at 12:15."

"Thank you, Shelby," I said.

"How are you?" she did something unusual and out of character; she sat on my bed. She put her head in her hands and wiped her forehead, face, and eyes. The fatigue was clear.

"I am a mess, Carly," she said.

I asked, "Why was Gwen up here? What was she doing?"

Shelby confessed, "She was with me. We stole a moment away since you were out." Shelby was extremely bereft.

"Gwen is - was my wife," Shelby said and let out deep sobs.

She was overcome. I put my arms around her.

"I had no idea," I said. It dawned on me why keeping this job was so important to Shelby. I offered to stay on the Estate, but Shelby asked me to go. She needed time to rest. Under my breath, I repeated Renee's words,

"What is happening?"

Shelby and I agreed to talk after the races. I changed my clothes and met Dalton downstairs. I felt Renee's sadness and Shelby's loss and deep pain. I felt George's concern and worry. I felt Judy's turmoil and uncertainty. I felt Jonah's affection and Morty's love. I felt Raul's jealousy and Mr. Hines' desire to do his job well. I realized that with Michael's death, I was alive to the world and the people around me. When Michael was alive, my awareness revolved around my own safety and self-defense. I was in "survival mode." Now that Michael's abuse no longer consumed me, I could feel love and compassion again -- and all the other feelings that come along with being awake. It was overwhelming and, at the same time, rewarding. Shouldn't I feel shame?

Mr. Hines and George were in our box with Jonah when I arrived. Jonah stood and greeted me with a kiss on the cheek. George embraced me, and Mr. Hines shook my hand.

Jonah said, "You look wonderful, Carly, despite the trying times."

"You flatter me, Doctor," I said.

"I'm sorry I took your gelding out of the sixth," he said.

I glanced at George, "Sorry, dear, I forgot to tell you."

Jonah explained, "He had stiffness in work-outs yesterday, and this race wouldn't benefit him, win or lose. I thought rest was best."

"I seconded that," George said.

"Well, I'm lucky you two are watching out for my interests," I said.

Marlene took our drink orders. Jonah ordered a Perrier, George ordered a draft, and I ordered wine. Mr. Hines excused himself to attend to security obligations. Jonah moved over one chair and sat next to me. George advised Jonah to bet on the seven. Jonah disagreed due to muscle atrophy in both front legs. Jonah instead suggested that the four-horse was a good bet. George nodded and left the box to place his bets.

"Alone, at last," Jonah quipped. "At least I won't be thrown to the ground this meeting."

Jonah was good company. George returned to the box, and Jonah stood to go, "I'm betting on our horses, George."

George winked at me and said, "Go get'em, Doctor."

"Carly, do you want to place a bet?"

"Yes," I said.

"I'd like a two, six quinella."

Jonah and George raised their eyebrows in surprise.

"An independent woman," George laughed as Jonah took my two dollars and left the box.

Chapter Twenty-One

I switched from wine to Perrier by the fourth race. George was right; the races were a good distraction, but he and I worried, nonetheless. Dr. Mortimer kept us updated on Renee's status by phone. She slept most of the day, waking only for sips of water and bathroom needs. I visited the Winner's Circle three times with George and the team. Photos were taken, and I was given copies. Jonah kept me company under the watchful eye of Mr. Hines through the twelfth race. When the day was over at Merit Downs, Dalton was waiting to take me home. Jonah walked me to the limo and kissed my cheek.

He said, "See you soon, Carly. My love to Renee."

I hugged Dalton, who was surprised by the gesture but returned the hug and said, "Thank you, ma'am."

As we drove back, I looked at the photos of our team in the Winner's Circle: George, Jonah, Raul, Jim, Pablo, and myself. There was another gentleman in each picture whom I did not recognize. I would ask George when he returned to the house. My mind shifted to Renee and Shelby. Gwen's loss, after Michael's loss, was tragic for them. I sighed deeply and asked the universe for some comfort and relief from pain. Were the deaths in Merit my fault? Was tragedy in other people's lives the punishment for my sins? I shuttered and shook off the thought.

At the Estate, I rang for Shelby. She did not respond, and I rang again. The phone rang in my room.

"Hello," I said.

"Ma'am," said Emily, "Shelby is in her quarters. She's been there all day."

"Thank you, Emily," I said, "Where are her quarters?"

I was embarrassed that I did not know. Emily gave me directions and inquired if I wanted dinner. I asked her to bring a fruit and cheese tray to Shelby's quarters. I changed into sweats and headed for the basement. I was reminded of the immense size of this house: Three floors and a basement. The ground floor included a large foyer; the dining room seated 40. There was the study, library, den, office, food storage area and kitchen. Three ample living spaces were on the second and third floors, and three bathrooms on each level. A separate elevator led to the third floor, for which only George, Renee, and Shelby had keys.

The employee's quarters were located in the basement. I had not been on the third floor, or down to the basement in my time on the Estate. Michael kept me on a short leash. As I approached the hallway leading to Shelby's suite, I passed the wine cellar and Emily and Dalton's quarters.

Emily met me with a snack tray and said, "I'll bring in tea."

I took the tray and knocked on Shelby's door. "Come in," she said in a whisper. Shelby was looking at photos of Gwen.

"Are you alright?" I asked.

"No," she answered. "I lost my wife and my life. Gwen was the most wonderful person, Carly. She was fun, kind, loving and gentle." Tears fell from Shelby's eyes.

I took her in my arms and held her as she wept. "I am sorry for your loss," I said.

I shared our snack tray with Emily when she brought the tea. Shelby did not have an appetite. We called Dr. Mortimer, who gave us an update on Renee. The Doctor reassured us that Renee would be home in a few days.

Emily asked if we wanted to exchange our tea for "something stronger." We agreed it was a good idea. She left and returned with four snifters and a bottle.

She said, "I called Dalton, and he's coming down." I laughed and felt a small slice of overwhelm dissipate with a moment of laughter. When Dalton arrived, I generously poured the Remy Martin Cognac.

Shelby said, "It's good to be bad."

We touched our glasses, toasted to Gwen, and took long sips of the soothing, smooth syrup. An hour passed as Shelby and Dalton shared stories of Gwen. Emily and I listened intently. I was sorry I did not have the opportunity to know her. I felt deep sympathy for Shelby and Renee. Dalton and Emily retired for the night, and I fell asleep at the foot of Shelby's bed.

Shelby woke me at five.

"Carly, you'd better go upstairs before George discovers you're gone."

She looked tired.

"What can I do for you today, Shelby?" I asked.

"Will you go into town and help me with Gwen's arrangements?"

"Of course," I said. "Just let me know when and what you need."

I held up an empty bottle and said, "Shelby, you'd better ask Maxine to order another bottle of Cognac for Renee. This one is toast."

Shelby said, "We did a number on that, didn't we? No wonder my head feels like I slept in a vice. I don't know how I'll go on, Carly" she said, sadly. I squeezed her arm and touched her cheek, "We will get through this, I promise."

I called Morty to ask about Renee. The phone went to voicemail, and I left a message. As I was getting ready to go to the hospital, Dalton called upstairs, "Carly, Dr. Silvers is here to see you."

"Oh? I'll be down in a few minutes," I said.

I finished dressing and joined Jonah in the Foyer. "Hello, Jonah," I said. "This is an unexpected surprise."

"Hello, Carly. How is Renee?"

"I haven't heard yet this morning, but it is nice of you to ask; always the gentleman," I said.

"I am going to the Ranges to assist with offloading the stock. I wondered if you'd like to join me? I hope it isn't too presumptuous, but the three of us went every year, and since Michael . . . well . . . I thought you might still like to go."

George came through the door. He kissed my cheek and shook Jonah's hand.

"Renee is still sleeping. I guess Dr. Mortimer knocked her out," he said.

"Rest is good," Jonah said.

George continued, "They're going to run routine tests to make sure nothing is going on that we don't know about, but the Doctor doesn't think there is; Renee will be home soon."

"Can she have visitors?" I asked.

"Dr. Mortimer advises against it. He said we all need a time-out. I am taking the opportunity to get some work done," he said.

Dr. Mortimer will be there as they run the tests. He wants the results right away. He will keep us informed. Good-day, you two; we'll talk later."

George got into the limo with Marc at the wheel and Maxine in the back.

Jonah was smiling.

"It looks like your schedule was just cleared."

"Let me change into my boots for the Ranges. I'll be right down," I said. I rang for Shelby, who was lost in sadness.

"I drank entirely too much cognac," she said.

I hugged her and asked if she was holding up. "I am lucky to have this job. Emily and Dalton are covering for me. Renee will be out for two more days, and George will be out today. I am getting the break I need."

"What time do you want to go into town?" I asked.

"We can't go today, Carly. Gwen is still at the M.E.'s office. The Mortuary will call when the M.E. transfers Gwen's body. Most-likely tomorrow." She began to cry, again. "I'm so sorry, my friend.

OK with you if I go with Jonah to the Ranges? If you want me to stay, I will."

"No," she said. "I will sleep – do you mind if I sleep in your bed, Carly? I don't want to be in the basement today."

"By all means," I said. I hugged her and promised to check in on her later in the day.

I changed into black cowboy boots and tucked my jeans inside. I threw on a black leather jacket. Jonah said, "Ready beautiful? Let's go talk to the animals. Just call me Dr. Doolittle."

His SUV felt different and somehow cozier than the limos and convertibles of the Estate. I was comfortable. I showed Jonah the picture taken at the track. I asked if he knew the stranger.

"I know him. He is an employee of Candiss Stables. I see him around the stalls and in the winner's circle. Is there a problem?"

"I don't know," I said. I shared my feelings about Renee, Fran, Judy, Gwen, and Shelby. Jonah was a thoughtful listener. Again, I was aware of his kind heart and attentiveness. He reached over and put his hand on mine.

He said, "Let it all go for now, Carly. Try to relax and let the day bathe you in a positive light."

I smiled and removed my hand to reach for a bottle of water. I took a long sip and wondered why his touch left me unsettled.

"Thank you. Good idea. I will," I said.

Chapter Twenty-Two

I enjoyed the ride to the Ranges, even though the train offloading site was fairly, far. Jonah was talking about the track and his daily obligations. It sounded rigorous. I had no idea he was at the track each day by four a.m. He discussed how the racing season put a strain on his ability to serve the community. He had taken on a temporary assistant to help-out through May.

"I love my job and the animals are my living. I get to know them and their habits and behaviors. That makes it easier to tell when something out of the ordinary is going on with them," he said. He talked about the way people love their animals, some more deeply than others. "I don't know what will happen to Mrs. Perkins when she loses that old sheep dog," he said. Jonah was a stark contrast to Michael.

When we arrived at the Ranges, all eyes were on Dr. Silvers.

I counted twelve, "Howdy, Doc's."

The hands addressed me with a tip of the hat and a timid "Mrs. Candiss." Everyone knew Michael. He was not well-liked, but he was well-known. Starla Beam threw her arms around me. She bounced me up and down.

"Hello, Mrs.," she said excitedly. "I thought I'd never see you again. Yes, ma'am. I am shore-ly glad to see you!" She shouted.

I flinched from her roughness but was happy to see her. She is the only woman in this tough group of scrappy men. She is a talented horsewoman and a hard-working hand. She is a modern-day "Calamity Jane." She also works the track; she loads the starting gate when needed and is a pony rider. In other words, she is one of the riders who leads the racehorses, and their jockeys onto the track and up to the starting gate. Starla and Jonah have been friends for years.

Dr. Silvers watched the unloading while the hands directed the stock into trucks and pens. He reviewed medical records for every bull, cow, calf, steer, boar, sow, and foul. He ran after two escapees with the help of Starla. The other men watched and cheered on the runaway turkeys. It was note-worthy that Jonah was well thought of and respected. I noticed two men walking in from a distance. They talked to Jonah, who was a good distance from me. He nodded in my direction, and they walked over.

"Hello, Mrs. Candiss," they said.

"Hello," I said hesitantly. "Who are you, and how can I help?"

They introduced themselves: Agent Brent and Agent Baxter. "We are with the FBI. Can we ask you a few questions?"

"I don't think I am supposed to answer questions without my lawyer present,".

Agent Brent replied, "If you are uncomfortable. You can choose not to answer."

I agreed.

Agent Baxter asked the first question. "Do you know Joanne Seeger?"

"Yes," I answered.

"Where do you know her from?"

"She is one of my husband's mistresses," I answered.

The agents seemed surprised and flashed a quizzical glance at one another. Agent Brent asked, "How long have you known her?"

"We have never met," I said. "I saw her last at my husband's funeral."

"Ma'am, do you know her brother?"

"Who is her brother?" I asked.

"Marc Seeger. Do you know him?"

"I don't think so," I said.

"Ma'am, you don't know George Candiss limo driver, Marc Seeger?"

"Oh, Marc, yes, I do, but I never knew his last name. Why do you ask?"

Agent Baxter said, "We can't say, ma'am, we are involved in several investigations. Your indulgence is appreciated."

"Of course," I said.

I showed them the photo. "Do you know that man?" I asked, pointing to the stranger.

"I don't," I said. Both agents denied knowing the man. They asked if they could keep the picture. Jonah walked over and put his arm around me.

"Can I do anything?" Agent Brent asked Jonah to wait at a distance while they asked a few more questions. Jonah agreed, but I did not. Agent Baxter said, "If you're ok with it."

"I am," I said. "Do you know Frances Durmont?"

"I know the woman who was hit by a car last week. If that is Frances Durmont, yes."

"And how long have you known her?"

"I met her the day before she was hit. She worked at my friend's salon. She washed my hair. I never met her before then."

Agent Brent asked, "How tall are you ma'am?"

"5'6"," I said.

"And approximately how much do you weigh?"

"Approximately 125," I answered.

I was about to object to answering questions about myself without my lawyer when Agent Baxter asked, "And what would you approximate the height of Fran?"

"5'6, or so," I said.

"And her weight?" he asked.

"130-135, I'd guess," I said.

"Ma'am, have you colored your hair recently?"

"No," I said. "I cut it, but no color."

I was unsettled by the question, "What is going on?" I asked.

Jonah interrupted and said, "I think that's enough, boys. Contact Bill Becker, Mrs. Candiss' Attorney, with anything further."

Jonah whisked me away.

"My hero," I joked. But when we started back to town, a sense of foreboding overtook me once again. I sobbed uncontrollably as I had in Judy's salon and in the hospital the day Fran was hit. I struggled to catch my breath. Jonah pulled over and came around to the passenger side of the SUV. He opened the door an helped me out.

He said, "Stand up straight – breathe in deeply – breathe in and out, Carly, in and out." He rubbed my back gently. "Breathe in and breathe out, in and out – relax. You're fine," he said. "You're fine."

I was soon calmer. I went into Jonah's arms.

"Oh, Carly," he said, "I wish this wasn't happening. I wish life was easier. You deserve so much more."

I was touched and glad to have the support of a loving man and a good friend.

Jonah dropped me off at the hospital. I called Morty, who answered right away. "Hello, Mrs. Candiss," he said. "I am with Renee right now. Where are you?"

"I am here in the main lobby. Can I come up?"

"She would love that," he said. "Can you stop in the café and bring up two vanilla shakes?"

"I'll make that three," I said.

"Be there soon."

I juggled three shakes and my purse up the stairs to the third floor. Renee was happy to see me and so was Dr. Mortimer. Renee kissed my cheek and asked after Shelby.

"How is my Shelby?" Renee asked.

"She is holding up," I said. "I slept in her quarters last night. We had a drink too many and I fell asleep at the foot of her bed."

"She loved Gwen," Renee said. "I just don't know how she will get through."

"We will all get through together," I said.

Morty raised his milkshake and said, "I'll drink to that."

We touched our Styrofoam cups together. Renee said, "I'll drink to anything," and we shared a spontaneous chuckle.

After our shakes, Renee drifted off and Morty encouraged me not to disturb her. He led me to the physician's quarters. He took me in his arms and pulled me close. "I have been thinking of our time together. It is almost unbearable to be apart. I had forgotten the magic between us and how good you feel and . . ." He kissed me again. I could feel his body respond to our touch. He was hungry for me. We dropped onto the bed. "Morty," I sighed, "Don't stop, Don't stop. I was overcome.

Chapter Twenty-Three

I told Morty about the FBI and how they questioned me about Joanne and Fran. Morty was more interested in my time with Jonah.

"Are you jealous?" I asked, "Morty, I am talking about being questioned by the FBI. Why your interest in Jonah? You know that Dr. Silvers, Michael, and I went to the Ranges every year when the stock arrived."

"I know, Carly, but you've been seeing him a lot lately," he said.

"This from the man who stood me up on opening day to have an all-night tryst with another man," I said angrily.

"Yes, and from a man who killed your husband!" he snapped back. My heart sank.

"Morty, why are we fighting?"

He took me in his arms, "We must be careful, darling. We must talk to one another. You're right; I have no right to be jealous, and I'm sorry. It's the passion you stir inside me," he admitted. "I've never felt this way for a woman -- forgive me."

Dr. Mortimer was called away. I showered in the physician's quarters and called Dalton. When he arrived, he was slightly disheveled. The last several weeks has taken its toll on all of us.

"Where to, ma'am?" he asked wearily.

"Dalton, would you call Angelo's and order two ultimate pizzas, please? Let's stop at Pete's and pick up some ice cream, too." I saw Dalton's face light up as he nodded in the rearview. "Do you know what flavor Emily and Shelby would like?"

"Yes, ma'am," he said as he placed the pizza order and drove to Pete's.

I stayed in the limo to give Dalton and Ellen a few minutes alone, "Dalton, I need to make a few phone calls. Do you mind if I wait here?"

"Of course, ma'am," he said.

He had a bounce in his step as he entered the ice cream parlor.

I dialed Judy's number. She did not pick up. I left a message, "Please call me if you can. I want to know how you are. You are my friend, and I love you."

I dialed Morty's number. No answer. I left a message. "Dr. Mortimer, this is Carly Candiss. I would like to have a meeting with you in the physician's quarters tomorrow if you are not too busy." I hung up with a broad smile on my face and a yearning for a repeat sexual interlude: The ultimate de-stressor, I thought to myself. I called the house, and Emily answered. "Hi Emily, Dalton and I are heading back, and we are bringing pizza and ice cream, so don't make dinner. Is there beer in the house?" I asked.

"Yes, ma'am, always beer in the house."

"Ok. See you soon."

Dalton returned with the ice cream, and we drove to Angelo's and picked up two deep-dish ultimate pizzas with extra cheese. We could hardly wait to get to the house to eat. They smelled so good. Shelby and Emily set the table with paper plates and the trophy goblets left over from opening day. We were like kids having a pizza party while our parents were away. My life felt normal. How could that be?? Was I in denial?

"Emily," Dalton said, "We got you German Chocolate Cake ice cream, and Shelby, we got you Mint Chocolate Chip."

"MMMMM," Shelby said.

"Ma'am," Dalton said, "I got you Jamoca Almond Fudge, right?"

"Exactly, Dalton and please call me Carly," I said.

Emily brought in four beers, and we all poured them into the trophy goblets. We raised our goblets, and Shelby said, "To Gwen and Renee."

We all repeated loudly, "To Gwen and Renee," and clinked or clunked our goblets. The cold beer went down easily, and the pizza was just what we needed.

I pulled out my phone and retrieved the pictures of the winner's circle the day before. Emily opened and distributed a second bottle of beer. I handed the photos to the staff as we polished off the pizza and asked, "Who is that man behind Raul?" Emily and Shelby did not know.

Dalton said, "He works for Mr. Candiss. Michael hired him last year – his name is Rosario."

"Michael hired him?" I asked.

"Yes, ma'am. I mean, Carly. Rosario watches over the Candiss' stable when all other eyes are busy elsewhere. He stays with the horses and watches over the stalls." I was intrigued.

"Isn't there security in place?" I asked.

"Yes, but the security team watches all the stables and all the stalls, so there are times when the Candiss Stable is unmanned. After Sweet Smith died in his stall last year, Michael did not want to take any chances."

"How did he die?" I asked.

"I thought Dr. Silvers said it was from an uncontrolled bleed following a race."

"Well," Dalton said, "Michael was afraid there was more to it than that."

I made a mental note to ask Jonah. Emily left the dining room and came in with four gallons of ice cream and four spoons. Shelby, was doing the best she could, but wearing her loss in plain view.

She said, "I miss Gwen more than I can say. I feel like my heart has gone missing."

The three of us listened as she talked about their wedding day twelve years before. Again, I marveled at my ignorance. How could I be so blind to these wonderful people who surround me? It was another long night. Shelby slept in my room. She did not want to be alone.

As morning light crept in, I was awakened by a loud clap of thunder. I saw lightning light up dark clouds to the North. No races today, I thought. The rain would be here soon. I called Judy again. No answer. Shelby returned with the newspaper and some coffee. I opened the terrace doors and the wind blew too hard to keep them open. I closed them and went downstairs to the dining room with the newspaper.

"Have you heard anything from the mortuary?" I asked Shelby.

She shook her head, "No."

"Come into Merit with me, Shelby, and we'll visit Renee."

"I couldn't," she said.

"I have work to do."

"It can wait," I insisted. Shelby smiled for the first time in days.

"Let me change," she said.

I called Dalton and asked him to bring the car around. I let Emily know and asked her to join us. She declined, saying someone needed to be at the Estate.

Shelby came upstairs wearing blue jeans and a pull-over sweater that fit her nicely. She put on some make-up and tied her hair back. She was a beautiful young woman. I was sorry for her loss and sorrier that my evil husband harmed her. She was a friend whom I had come to like very much. Emily came to the door with a brown corduroy jacket.

"You might need this," Emily said.

Shelby hesitated, "No, I couldn't."

Emily gently encouraged Shelby, "Take it." With tears, Shelby agreed and put on the jacket.

"This was Gwen's favorite," she said. I took Shelby's arm, and we walked to the car where Dalton was waiting.

"Let's go see Renee," I said.

The skies opened-up on our ride into Merit. There was a spectacular light show and loud thunder. Large drops of rain hit the windshield, and the windshield wipers worked overtime.

Dalton said, "There are umbrellas in the bin, under the passenger side bench."

I retrieved two.

"Thank you, Dalton. You always think ahead."

"Thank you for noticing," he said.

It felt good to have these people in my life. I only wish it hadn't taken me so long to get to know them. I reflected on my departure from the Estate. I would truly miss them. Shelby was quiet. Her healing had not begun. She was raw and bereft. I put my hand in hers. She was startled.

"I hope you don't mind," I said.

Tears fell from her eyes. She shook her head, "No. I don't mind. Thank you, Carly."

We settled back and watched the storm. That's what I felt like I was doing in my life – watching the storm and waiting for it to pass.

I called Morty and told him that Shelby and I were just arriving at the hospital.

"Good," he said, "I got your message."

"Maybe Shelby and Renee will want to visit alone a little."

"Perhaps," I said.

We took the stairs to the third floor. Renee was just finishing breakfast.

She burst into tears, "My girls!" she shouted.

She took Shelby into a long embrace, and Shelby cried in Renee's arms. I hugged and kissed Renee and took a trophy goblet from my purse. I poured her ice water into the goblet.

"There," I announced loudly – "A cup fit for a winner."

We giggled through tears.

Chapter Twenty-Four

Morty came into Renee's room.

"Carly, can I speak with you about the neurologist appointment?" he asked.

I looked at Renee and Shelby and said, "OK with you two if I step out?"

Renee said, "Take your time, dear."

Morty led me to the physician's quarters. He kissed me gently. It felt right and wonderful. He pulled me against him, kissing me softly. He lifted my blouse and unfastened my bra. He softly kissed my breasts. I moaned. He undid my jeans. He put his hands on my hips as he pushed his hips forward.

"OH, Carly," he gasped.

I gave myself to him with a long, trembling moan. Afterward and breathlessly, I asked, "Can we feel this good? Aren't we sinners who deserve to be punished? Is it possible to move forward and be happy?"

Morty kissed me, "I think so, my darling."

Morty and I cleaned up and went back to Renee's room. Renee and Shelby were playing rummy. Renee said, "You know I'd forgotten what it's like to sit still. It can be quite fun."

Morty whispered, "It's the drugs."

I could tell Shelby had been crying. Renee said, "I want to pay for all of the arrangements for Gwen, Carly. Will you see to it?"

"Of course, Renee," I said.

Shelby burst into tears again. "Thank you, thank you," she sobbed. "You are so kind."

I walked over to Shelby and rubbed her back as she cried into Renee's hospital gown.

Dr. Mortimer said, "Ok, you three, that's enough for one day. Renee needs to rest and Shelby -- Dr's orders -- You do too. I am writing you a prescription for rest."

"Can you add some Chocolate Mint ice cream?" I asked.

We hugged Renee and left to find Dalton.

As we exited the hospital, I caught a glimpse of the two FBI agents who questioned me at the Ranges. They were in plain clothes, leaving the lobby and walking toward the M.E.'s office next door. They did not see me. I was still unnerved about their investigation. I had received no word from my lawyer. There had been nothing in the paper about Roger or Fran. I was sure it was because of the need for forensics to be completed.

Once we were outside, Shelby sadly said, "The mortuary called while you were with Dr. Mortimer. Gwen is there now, and they would like me to come in."

"Do you want to go now?" I asked.

"Yes," she said.

Dalton drove us to Fairchild's Mortuary. We were met by Mr. Fairchild's daughter, Deena, who was professional and sensitive.

She hugged Shelby and said, "I am so sorry, Shel. You must be destroyed. Gwen loved you so much."

Shelby had tears rolling down her cheeks.

"This is Carly Candiss."

Deena looked surprised. She shook my hand, "Mrs. Candiss, it's nice to meet you."

"Likewise," I said. "I wish it were under better circumstances -- and please -- call me Carly."

Deena asked Shelby, "Do you want to see her?"

Shelby nodded.

I asked, "Do you want to go alone?"

Shelby shook her head. I wrapped my hands around her upper arm and said, "OK."

Deena led us to a small room with an open casket and two sofas.

"Just push the button when you're ready, and I'll come back."

I let go of her arm, and Shelby walked to the casket. She looked at her lovely wife and said, "Oh, Gwen, come back to me, please. I can't live without you."

Shelby sobbed. She asked, "What happened? How did you fall?"

Shelby was overcome with grief. Her phone rang, and she handed it back to me. I left the room, "Hello?"

"Shelby, this is Maxine; how are you?"

"This is Carly," I said, "we are at the mortuary."

"Oh, good, Carly. Thank you for being there, stay with her, please. George has been relentless with Renee out. He is like a twenty-year-old. The problem is I'm still 45," she said.

I felt myself blush. Maxine had never before spoken to me in such a personal manner. It seemed I was now part of the family.

I returned to the room with Shelby. She was on the sofa.

"That was Maxine," I said. I walked to the coffin. Gwen's face was pale and peaceful. I sat with Shelby, and an hour passed.

"Would you call Deena?" Shelby asked. She was quiet and calm. I pushed the button, and Deena came in a few minutes later. We left Gwen and went into the office. Deena went over Shelby's options and costs. I told Shelby not to worry about the cost. Shelby said, "Gwen didn't want a funeral; she wanted a celebration. She didn't want to be buried. She wanted to be cremated, and her ashes poured over East Lake from a plane. She wanted the song, 'Now and Forever,' by Carole King, played at her celebration."

Deena took Shelby in her arms. "Oh, my friend, I am sorry." Shelby seemed safe and comforted by Deena's caress.

We left the Mortuary, and I was ashamed to be starving. "Shelby, can we stop for a bite? Would you mind?" The rain was still pouring down. "I know you don't feel like eating, but perhaps a strong drink would help?" She reluctantly agreed. "Dalton, will you take us to the Waymark?" I asked.

"Yes, Ma'am," he said.

"Join us for a drink?" I asked.

"No, ma'am. I'm driving."

Oscar greeted us warmly with hand-shakes and air kisses. "Shelby, darling, I was so sorry to hear. If you need anything sweet thing, you just call Uncle Oscar," he said. He led us to the Candiss table and asked, "Drinks?" I asked for red wine, and Shelby asked for a Bombay Gin Martini. "And keep them coming, Oscar."

Shelby was looking at and touching her Jacket. She said, "Carly, there is so much I want to tell you."

"You can start as soon as we get our drinks," I said.

"Thank you, Carly, for not hating me for what I did before, you know."

Oscar appeared with our drinks. I said, "Listen, Shelby, every one of us did things with and for Michael that we never should have. He was an evil man."

I ordered a fish sandwich and fries with a cup of soup. Shelby ordered a cup of soup and a second martini. I asked about Deena.

Shelby said, "I've known the Farichilds for years. Deena and I went to school together. The only fight Gwen and I had was about Deena. Gwen thought Deena made a pass at me at Renee's opening-day reception a few years ago. Gwen was incensed." Shelby laughed, "But Deena didn't, Carly, she asked if I knew if GWEN was seeing anyone. When Gwen questioned me, I didn't want to say an attractive younger woman had the hots for her. When she finally forced the truth out of me, Gwen said, 'Honey, don't you know -- you are my soulmate?'"

Our food arrived. Shelby ordered a third Martini. I ate like they were going to take away my plate. Shelby became ultra-talkative.

She asked, "Why did you marry Michael?"

"I was young. He was handsome and powerful. He made me love him. It was a game, and I was his pawn."

"We were all game pieces on Michael's chess board," Shelby slurred. "Gwen hated Michael for what he made me do, Carly. She wanted to poison him."

"SHHH," I said. "Shelby!"

"She did, Carly. She wanted him dead. A lot of people did." I ordered coffee. Shelby pouted. "Does that mean no more Martini's?" she asked.

"I think you've had enough," I said.

"Talk to the staff, Carly. You don't know the half of Michael's escapades. He kept you in the dark intentionally. Everyone covered for him, especially Raul," she said. "Talk to Raul. We think HE killed Michael."

"Drink your coffee, Shelby," I cautioned.

"Whatever would make Raul want to kill Michael?" I asked.

"Talk to Raul," she said.

I was confused. What could I learn from Raul?

Chapter Twenty-Five

On the drive home, Shelby fell asleep right away. Her head dropped into my lap, and I smiled tenderly at her.

"Poor girl," I said out loud.

Dalton said, "Yes, poor girl."

We drove through heavy rain until we reached the Estate. Dalton and I helped Shelby to her feet and supported her as we made our way inside. Emily met us at the door and helped me get Shelby downstairs. Shelby was singing, "Now and forever." She said, "I will die missing Gwen." We undressed Shelby, put on her nightgown, and dropped her into bed. I was about to leave the room and Shelby began to cry. Emily excused herself, and I sat with Shelby. "Stay with me," she begged. I don't want to be alone."

"OK," I said, "but let me change my clothes." I went to my room, showered quickly, and changed into my nighty."

I walked back down to Shelby's quarters and found her fast asleep. I turned on her TV and settled in next to her. I understood her need to have company. I drifted off.

I woke several hours later to the softest kiss and most gentle touch. Shelby ran her hands across my shoulders and down my chest. My first impulse was to stop her, but I did not. She kissed my lips as If she wanted to feel their texture. She rubbed her soft cheek against my face and touched her eye lashes to mine and her forehead to mine. She kissed me softly. She slowly moved her lips down my neck. She lightly kissed my breasts and ran her hand down my thigh. I softly moaned. She said, "Gwen." She rocked gently. She kissed me tenderly. I was overcome with guilty pleasure. I began to move my hips. She moaned, "Yes." I shuttered. Shelby rolled halfway onto the bed and fell fast asleep, with her head resting on my shoulder . . .

I left her room.

In the morning, I woke to the phone ringing. It was Judy. She asked, "Who is Rosario?"

"What? Who is this?" I asked.

"It's Judy," she replied and repeated, "Who is Rosario?"

"He is a stable hand and stall guard at the track," I said.

"Well, turn on the news. He was just arrested for Roger's murder." I leaped out of bed. Judy said, "Quick, Carly, Channel 7."

I turned it on in time to see Rosario in handcuffs, as they placed him in the back of a patrol car. "What is going on?" I asked.

"Apparently, he was questioned by the FBI and confessed, but there is more, Carly. They are looking for two suspects. A man and a woman who posed as you and Michael at a bank in Cater six months ago. They had your IDs and your bank account numbers, but the teller felt something wasn't right. She called the manager, and they fled. Carly, the grainy video from the bank looks like you and Michael."

I was perplexed, "Let's talk later," I said.

I jumped off the bed just as Shelby came in with coffee. "Shelby, they just arrested someone for the murder of Roger Stiles," I shouted.

"Thank God," she said.

"Have coffee with me on the terrace," I said. She looked particularly downtrodden. "What's up?" I asked.

"Carly, I am so sorry about last night; I was drunk and heartbroken. I shouldn't have . . . " I stopped her by putting my finger to her lips. "SHHHH."

I kissed her gently and said, "Are you kidding? Last night was awesome. Say no more."

Shelby joked, "Why, Mrs. Candiss, there is a lot I never knew about you."

"You and me both," I said.

"Let's call it two friends who were there for one another in crisis."

Shelby smiled, hugged me tightly, and said, "Gwen would approve of that, Carly. Thank you."

We kissed again. I was happy to have her as my friend. I felt no more guilt. I thought about Morty and Raul. I understood a little better.

I called Dr. Mortimer. "How is Renee," I asked.

"She is chomping at the bit to come home," he said. "Her tests were normal, despite some elevated liver enzymes, which is normal for an alcoholic. She can come home tomorrow. I promised George not to let her out too soon. She's been a handful since Michael's death."

"So, you two are in Cahoots?" I asked.

"He pays my bills and besides, Renee needed rest, which she got here."

"When can we meet?" I asked.

He answered, "Come here, darling. I can't get you off my mind."

How could I refuse? I was anxious to tell him about Rosario. "Give me an hour," I said. I showered and rinsed with apple spice body wash. I put on a braless, backless long dress. I intentionally omitted underwear. Sex was enjoyable when it was consensual. It felt good to be this alive.

Dalton drove me to the hospital. He was talkative. I was getting used to the staff talking after all the years of silence. Dalton explained the guard shacks and how the staff rotated. He explained the cameras and the footage that George kept or discarded. Dalton explained that George's main interest was the horse's health and well-being, as well as monitoring the grounds. I asked him to elaborate. He timidly went on, "Well, ma'am -- Carly – your husband was the problem. He made enemies and had questionable affiliations. He hired stable hands he refused to pay. He had them pick horses, and he covered their bets. If they won, they kept the winnings. If not – no pay. He had dark affiliations, as well. That's why he hired Rosario. There were too many people with vendettas at the track. He only paid one jockey – Pablo. The others got paid in limited bar tabs, meals and sleeping quarters. If you'll excuse me, ma'am, your husband was a bastard."

"Dalton, why would Rosario kill Roger?" I asked, "and did he kill Fran?"

"I don't think so," Dalton explained. "They lived together. Rosario got Fran the job at the salon through Roger. If you ask me, all of this is about corruption, money, and who knew what about whom?"

"What about Gwen," I asked.

"Excuse me, Carly?"

I asked again, "What about Gwen? Who would want to kill Gwen?"

Dalton was shocked. "It was an accident, Carly. She fell downstairs. She was looking at her phone and wearing shitty heels."

"Did you see her?" I asked.

"No, I was out with Maxine getting the box seats cleaned for the Waymark staff's discount day."

"Did anyone see Gwen fall?" I asked.

"No. Emily was in the kitchen. Shelby was on the third floor of the residence, cleaning. Renee was in the den, and George was in his office."

"Where was Marc?" I asked.

"I don't know."

"Dalton, do you think you could check the tapes without arousing suspicion?"

"Yes."

"Would you check that night and see where Marc was?"

"Yes, and I could check the guard shack sign-in sheets."

"OK," I said, "but be careful and keep this between us."

I called Morty and told him I was in the hospital. He was already in the physician's quarters waiting. He was eager for my visit. When I walked in, he said, "Lock the door." He removed the newspaper from his lap, revealing a gift for me. "I've been like this since we spoke." I stared at his gift.

"I have a surprise for you, too," I said. I pulled up my dress, straddled his lap, and lowered myself onto him. "Me too," I said. "How did we ever wait so long?"

We offered up our passion to one another's desire. It was quick and intense. Morty said, "Now I'll want you whenever I eat apple pie. As a matter of fact, I would like some now."

Chapter Twenty-Six

After a shower and a kiss, Dr. Mortimer and I went to see Renee. She was having her nails done.

"Hello, dears," she said.

"I hear you're getting sprung tomorrow," I said.

"Yes, dear, it seems we are both free to roam about the country. I think I deserve a river cruise, and you and Shelby should come along. We'll live in luxury, eat out, and take in the sights and sounds of the river. It will be a marvelous way to forget our worries."

"What about the Estate, Renee? Can it get along without you and Gwen?" I asked.

"Maxine, George, Raul, and Emily can handle it," she said.

"What about Marc?" I asked, "Won't he help?"

"Haven't you heard, dear? He no longer works on the Estate. He took a job with the Candiss Corporation in Texas." I made a mental note to tell Dalton.

Morty told Renee she could be picked up after 11 the next morning.

"I'll come and get you with Dalton," I said.

"Bring Shelby, and we'll go to the track for lunch," Renee said happily. "And Carly, bring the black pant suit from the cleaners next to Hattie's, will you, please? I'm having my hair done this afternoon. I'll be ready when you get here."

Dr. Mortimer said, "Now, ladies, go easy on the liquor tomorrow. It doesn't mix well with the meds."

"Oh, Dr.," Renee replied, "I have been cooped up for days."

"Okay, Renee, just don't overdo it. I know how you Candiss women are," he said. "You go above and beyond."

I blushed, "Yes, we like to prove our worth, don't we, Renee?"

"Well, yes," she said, "we do."

I kissed her goodbye, and Morty walked me to the door.

"What did you want to talk to me about?" he asked.

"Will we see each other once Renee is out? How will we manage that?" I asked.

"We'll figure it out."

"I wanted to ask you about Raul. I heard that he had an intense dislike for Michael but did unscrupulous things for Michael. Is that true?"

"That is a conversation for wine and another day -- It's complicated." He guided me to the front door and said, "I'll see you later."

Dalton was at the curb. I got in and asked him to stop by the cleaners next to Hattie's. He asked if he could get me a coffee. "Sure, that would be great. Thanks, Dalton."

I went in and picked up Renee's cleaning. I was about to walk out, and the attendant asked, "Would you like Michael's clothes, Mrs. Candiss?"

I was taken aback. "Yes," I said.

He handed me the hanger and said, "I'm sorry we were unable to get the blood out. Pity, though, it's a nice suit."

"Yes, it is a nice suit. It was one of my favorites," I said.

I covered Michael's suit with Renee's clothes and walked to the limo.

Dalton was coming out of Hattie's. He said, "Are you all right, Carly? You look like you've seen a ghost."

"Dalton," I said, "Can we stop at the Travel Spot, please? And would you mind asking Jenna for brochures on river cruises?"

"Yes, Mrs. Candiss," he said. "Dalton, will you call me Carly?"

"Old habits, ma'am," he said, and we both chuckled.

We drove home in silence as I pretended to look through the brochures. My mind was on Raul, Gwen's death, and the blood on Michael's suit. Is it my blood? Should I get rid of the suit? Would it matter, now that Michael is dead? When did Michael last wear that suit?

"Hurry up, Shelby," I groused as she finished my make-up. "Renee wants us there by 11."

"Stay still," Shelby demanded.

Emily walked in with assorted Danish and doughnuts and said, "You two sound like sisters."

"What a nice thing to say," I said. "I never had a sister."

Emily joked, "And ya' had to pick this one?" We all laughed. "You two have fun today. Try to forget the heartaches," she said as she left the room.

"Do you think we will ever forget the heartaches?" she asked.

"No," I said.

"Do you think Emily feels left out?" Shelby asked.

"No," I replied. "She seems to be happy to stay on the Estate. She is detail-oriented; I think she takes her job fairly seriously."

"Let's bring something home for her," Shelby suggested.

"Yes. We can stop at the smell-good boutique," I said. Shelby was concerned for the welfare of others, even in her own grief. I loved that about her.

We arrived at the hospital at 11 on the dot. Renee was in the bathroom. Shelby and I had our hair done make-up on, and we were dressed for the occasion.

Dr. Mortimer said, "Wow. Those men at the track don't stand a chance." Shelby blushed. "Excuse me, Shelby," he said. ". . . Neither do the women."

We all laughed as I knocked on the bathroom door and handed Renee's suit in. In a few short minutes, Renee came out with a loud "Ta-Da!" She twirled around so we could see her hair.

"Renee," Shelby shouted, "It's pink!"

"Looks just like cotton candy, doesn't it?" Renee laughed.

"It's different," I said, "but it's a very pretty color."

Renee said, "Well, I love it. I am going to keep it this color."

Dr. Mortimer whispered, "It's the meds. Please be careful today."

Shelby and I promised.

"I pass," Renee said.

The track was bustling as the crowd formed lines to place their bets. The announcer changed some Jockey's for the day, corrected morning-line odds and weights, and relayed information on eliminations. George was in the box with Maxine, Jonah, and Mr. Hines. Hector was standing outside the box, talking to George about possible winners for the day.

George looked in our direction and whistled, "Now, here comes trouble," he said. He greeted Renee with a warm hug and kiss, "Hello, darling, are you feeling better?"

"I am fit as a fiddle," she replied.

George hugged Shelby next, "Anything you need, dear, just tell us." George turned his attention to me, "My daughter-in-law," he said, "my son was no fool." He kissed my cheek and helped me into the box with the others.

Maxine, Jonah, and Mr. Hines greeted all of us but paid special attention to Shelby. Their condolences, kindness, and warm wishes were authentic. Shelby was moved – as was I – by the compassion of our friends and family. Jonah kissed my cheek and embraced me gently.

"Mrs. Candiss, you are beautiful as ever."

"Thank you, Jonah," I said, "and you are still the gentleman."

I motioned to Mr. Hines, and he shook my hand.

"Mr. Hines, I would like to talk with you if you don't mind."

"Of course, Mrs. Candiss, better for me after the fourth, all right?" he asked.

"That will be fine, thank you," I said.

Maxine nodded in my direction and smiled. She hugged Shelby and sat down next to her. Marlene took our drink orders. We all ordered wine, except Renee, who ordered "whiskey," and Jonah, who ordered "Perrier."

Jonah sat next to me with his arm on the back of my chair. He said, "Rosario was arrested. Isn't that who you asked me about the other day?"

"Yes," I admitted. "I gave his picture to the FBI. Do you think that had anything to do with his arrest?"

"Well, I'd think so," he said, "they questioned him for some reason."

Jonah dropped his arm from the back of my chair onto my shoulder, "These are troubling times. How are you holding up?" Jonah was always eager to show me care and concern.

"I am doing ok," I said. I looked at Shelby and Renee, "I have good friends."

"I hope I am on that list," he said.

"You are," I answered. "Can you tell me about Sweet Smith?"

Jonah frowned, "An untimely death, Carly. He bled internally after a mile race. I wasn't here, and one of the hands put the horse on the hot walker without examination. When I arrived, it was too late. It was unfortunate."

Chapter Twenty-Seven

After the fourth race, I excused myself and made my way to Security. Mr. Hines was exiting the office as I arrived.

"There you are, Mrs. Candiss, how can I help?"

"Mr. Hines," I said, "Can you tell me why Michael hired Rosario?"

Mr. Hines shook his head, "Your husband, ma'am, displayed some paranoia around the track. He was hypervigilant about his horses. Don't you agree?"

"Mr. Hines, I was not aware of my surroundings when Michael was alive."

"I understand, Ma'am," he said in a sympathetic manner. "Your husband bred contempt. He was unscrupulous and cruel. He hired Rosario to watch the stalls and remain at the stable."

"Why did Rosario kill Roger?" I asked.

"We think it had to do with money, Ma'am."

"Money?" I asked.

"Yes, unpaid and extensive gambling debt," he said. "We'll find out, ma'am."

"And Fran?" I asked.

"We'll find that out too."

Mr. Hines walked me back to the box. "Have you talked to Judy Stiles?" he asked.

"I have," I said, "she told me you were a good friend who could be trusted."

"That's true, and she needs more friends to trust," he said sympathetically. "Roger's death and Fran's murder have been hard on her."

"And hard on all of us," I said. "Mr. Hines, could Gwen's death be a part of all of this?"

He looked down but did not answer. "Again, Mrs. Candiss, we never had this conversation." He tipped his hat and started to walk away.

"Mr. Hines, what do you know about Marc Seeger?"

He was surprised. "Mrs. Candiss," he said, "let the FBI and the police do their jobs. Don't ask questions that may put you in harm's way. What we know is that someone has something to hide, and they're willing to kill to keep it a secret."

Dr. Mortimer had joined the party. He changed from scrubs into a teal shirt with black and teal tie and black trousers. He was seated in front of Shelby and a chair away from Jonah. I sat between them. Morty jumped up and yelled, "Come on, come on, girl, come on . . . Yes!" His bet paid off. He cheered, turned and hugged me and kissed my cheek. He joked, "You brought me good luck!"

George looked at his ticket and dropped it to the ground. "I lost," he said. "Why didn't you bring me good luck?"

Morty left to claim his winnings, and Jonah once again put his arm on my chair. He moved closer to me, "I am the lucky one," he said. "Look at the beautiful women I am surrounded by."

Shelby, Renee, and I took a bathroom break. Again, I saw the two FBI agents. They were coming from security-carrying videos. They saw me as we walked past and said, "Hello, Mrs. Candiss."

"Hello," I said.

Shelby was inquisitive, "Who was that, Carly?"

"FBI," I said flatly.

"Thank God," Renee said. "I hope they find justice for Roger and that poor girl who was hit by the car."

"Renee," I asked, "Did you know that Rosario and Fran lived together?"

"Who is Fran, dear?" she asked.

"The girl that was hit by the car," I said.

Renee stopped dead in her tracks, "I had no idea."

Shelby gasped, "No kidding?" We took a detour to the bar. "What is going on?" Shelby asked.

Renee was all ears.

"I'm not supposed to tell anyone, but Mr. Hines thinks someone is hiding something, and they are willing to kill to keep a secret."

"For goodness sake," Renee blurted out.

"Roger was most-likely killed over money," I said.

"By who?" Renee asked.

"That is the question," I said.

Renee ordered three drinks and went into the restroom. Shelby and I took the moment to embrace and share a friendly kiss. "Oh, Carly, I am glad to have you as my friend."

"Me too," I said, "I'm sorry our journey to friendship was long and hard." We looked at each other and grinned, "No pun intended," I said. "Shelby," I asked, "Did you drop off one of Michael's suits at the cleaners before he died?"

"No. That would be Marc or Dalton. They made all the cleaning runs because they were in and out of town every day. Why do you ask?"

"Oh, it's nothing," I answered.

When we arrived at the box, Morty and Jonah were gone. Maxine saw us coming and removed her hand from George's knee. "The two doctors were called away," George said. "And I have to take my lovely cotton-candy wife to the winner's circle." George took Renee by the hand and led her away. Shelby told Maxine what we were discussing at the bar.

Maxine said, "When I was at the salon a few weeks ago, Fran was talking with Roger in the breakroom. I couldn't hear what was said. I could tell Roger was angry. Judy told me Roger wanted to fire Fran, and Roger was the reason Judy hired her."

"Why?" Shelby asked.

Maxine shrugged, "Who knows? In my opinion, we should forget about Fran and Roger and move on with our lives. What's done is done."

"That's cold, Maxine," I said.

"Shelby, did you see Marc the day Gwen fell?" I asked.

"No, why?"

"Maxine, did you?"

Maxine thought about it, "I did. When Dalton and I left the Estate, we took two cars. I was a short distance away when I saw George's convertible. I knew

George was in his office, so I drove forward slowly until I saw that it was Marc. He must have come in the back gate."

"And you never saw Marc, Shelby?" I asked.

"No."

"Then where was he when Gwen fell? Shelby, who found Gwen?" I asked.

"Renee," she said. "I was in the residence when I heard her scream. I ran downstairs, and George was on the phone with 911. Renee was cradling my sweet Gwen."

Shelby wiped her tears, and Maxine asked, "So Marc wasn't there? He must have put the car in the garage and left the Estate."

"I never saw him," Shelby said, "do you think . . ., her words trailed off. Maxine seemed particularly interested in Marc's whereabouts.

George and Renee returned to the box. Shelby was inconsolable. I said, "I am going to take Shelby home. She needs to rest."

"Of course," Renee said and wiped Shelby's face. George called Dalton and told him Shelby and I were coming down. She was overwrought, "Oh Carly, could Marc have killed Gwen?"

Dalton helped us in the car.

"Dalton, did you know about Marc's resignation and transfer?" I asked.

He looked at me in the rear view, "No."

I took the card out of my purse and called Agent Baxter. I explained what was discussed at the track. He asked, "Where are you now?"

I asked Dalton to see Shelby back, and put her in Emily's hands and for the two of them to stay with her. Dalton dropped me at the police station to meet with the FBI.

Agent Baxter and Agent Brent arrived and, to my surprise, were accompanied by Mr. Hines. We made our way through an interesting crowd to an interrogation room. Mr. Hines started a recorder and asked, "Mrs. Candiss, for the record, have you been drinking?"

"Yes. I was at the track with my family. I had a few drinks over several hours."

Agent Baxter asked, "Would you say you are inebriated?"

"Not at all," I said.

The interview began. I told them all I knew, including Marc's unexpected relocation. They asked me about my husband.

"He was abusive and cruel," I said. "From what I have learned since his death, he was loathed. It seems Michael's redeeming quality was the insight into horses, unlike his insight into people. I'm sure Mr. Hines can verify."

"Mrs. Candiss, what can you tell us about the fist fight between your husband and Mark Seeger?"

"Nothing," I said, "I was unaware." I thought about the dry cleaning and the blood on Michael's suit.

I began to cry – it was real grief – for the ten years of my life, I would never get back. Mr. Hines and the Agents discussed a search warrant to view the videos and sign-in logs at the guard shacks. Were the murders of Fran and Roger related to Gwen's death? If so, why and who else might be in danger? Mr. Hines asked, "Carly, do you think Michael's death was part of this spider web?"

I looked him in the eye, "No. I do not, Mr. Hines. I was with Michael. We had a rough and spontaneous sexual encounter. He died on top of me. There was no one else involved in the last few moments of my husband's life. Prior to that moment, he was fine and entertaining a room full of admirers."

Mr. Hines nodded and seemed satisfied with my explanation. I wondered if he saw or felt my guilt.

Chapter Twenty-Eight

Mr. Hines drove me back to the Estate.

"What are you thinking?" I asked.

After a long pause, he said, "I was thinking about the race track, Carly. I was thinking about the mysterious deaths and who could be behind the deception. There is too much that doesn't add up."

"You'll figure it out," I said, "I have faith in you." I questioned him, "Mr. Hines, your appearance has changed, right?"

"Yes, Mrs. Candiss. I shaved my beard and lost sixty pounds. I was ambushed two years ago at the track and badly beaten. I didn't see the guys, and they were never caught. I was taken off guard and overpowered. I am in better shape now. That won't happen again."

"Any idea why?" I asked.

"Many," he replied and left it at that.

The house was quiet. I went directly to Shelby's quarters. Dalton, Emily, and Renee were there. They looked like teenagers who stayed up too late at a slumber party. They were eating ice cream out of cartons, and all of them looked pie-eyed.

"Oh, Carly, too bad you missed the cocktails," Renee slurred, "they were wonderful."

Dalton stood up and fell back against the wall.

"What did I miss?" I asked.

Renee held up an empty fifth of Four Roses and said, "I need to be excused." Emily was sitting on the bed, and Shelby was lying with her head on Emily's lap. Renee said, "Carly dear, you take over here. My husband is waiting for me to pass out so he can sneak out." She chuckled.

Dalton managed to lean forward, and the momentum allowed him to make it to the door. "Good night, everybody," he said.

"How did it go?" Shelby asked. "I told them what we discussed and everything I know. They're going to ask for videos and logs for the day Gwen fell."

Shelby clarified, "The day Gwen died."

I touched her cheek, "If they are not given up voluntarily, a search warrant will be issued," I said.

Emily spoke up, "I didn't see Marc that night, Carly. I went outside and waited for the ambulance and Mr. Candiss' convertible was not there. If it was, the firetruck couldn't have pulled in. If Marc came in, he wasn't here long, and he left in a hurry."

"Where is Gwen's tablet?" I asked. Shelby pointed to the dresser. "If no one saw her, then why does everyone say her fall was an accident?" I asked.

"It wasn't with her," Shelby said, pointing to the tablet. "When we found her, it wasn't there."

Emily's interest was piqued.

I grabbed the tablet. "Did the police look at this," I asked.

"I don't know," Shelby said.

"No," Emily said.

"I didn't see it. Mr. Candiss must have picked it up and set it on his desk when he went to the office to call 911. That's where I saw it last, but I didn't realize it was Gwen's. There was chaos, Carly. Gwen's phone was lying next to her and showed that she was on the phone at the time of her fall," Emily recalled.

"What's the password," I asked as I opened the tablet.

"Tweedle-dee 157," Shelby said, "and don't ask." We looked at the tablet and saw nothing out of the ordinary at first.

Emily said, "Check in audio recording or videos?"

I clicked on the video, but nothing. When I clicked on audio, Gwen's voice was frenetic, "What are you doing? Let go of me; Let me go!" There were sounds of a struggle, "Give that back – what are you . . ." The audio stopped. Shelby sat straight up, "OH MY GOD!" She yelled. I called Mr. Hines.

Mr. Hines came into the foyer with Agent Brent and Agent Baxter. George, Dalton, Shelby, Emily, and I were waiting. George started the discussion, "It seems that Gwen may have been a victim of a crime. He played the recording; we listened several times. The Agents took possession of the tablet. They served George a search warrant for the Estate videos and logs from the guard shacks. They also informed us they would question all the staff.

George said, "Of course, anything you need. We want to get to the bottom of this."

Mr. Hines shook my hand with genuine concern, "I hope we can bring this to a close for everyone's well-being."

Emily saw the agents at the door.

We were exhausted and went to our rooms to collapse. I was just drifting off when I heard a knock at the door. It was Shelby and Emily.

"Carly, can we sleep in here?" Shelby asked.

I said, "Yes, come in," and I rolled the covers back. Emily checked the doors on the terrace. They were locked. They crawled into bed. I was grateful for the king mattress that Michael insisted upon. I was unsettled after the discussion and new insight about Gwen's death. None of us felt particularly safe. Thanks to each other's company and physical and emotional exhaustion, we fell asleep quickly and slept well.

Morning found us wrapped in sunlight as Renee opened the doors to the terrace. "I was going to have breakfast brought up, but I couldn't find my staff this morning," she chuckled. "If I'd known there was a sleepover, I would have brought my long johns," she said cheerily. "And what did you girls do to poor Dalton?" she asked, smiling widely. I rolled over to see Emily still asleep and Shelby curled around Emily with her eyes barely open, looking at me.

"Climb in, Renee, or come back in half an hour," I said.

Renee left the room, "Breakfast, ladies . . . we need breakfast, soon . . . up and at 'em!" Renee cheered.

Shelby was the first to climb out of our snug, warm nest. She pulled Emily up by the arm. Emily looked at the clock and gasped, "Oh, Mr. Candiss will want his eggs. She flew into the bathroom."

Shelby walked around to my side of the bed. She leaned over and gently kissed my lips. "Good morning," she said, "and thank you, Carly."

She left the room to prepare for the day. Emily followed a few minutes later, "Breakfast in an hour," she said as she ran by. In that moment, I understood two things of which I never before had a grasp: One – how one woman could deeply love another; and two – how important the friendships of these women had become.

After breakfast, Renee and George appeared on the terrace as I was finishing my coffee. George had updated Renee on last night's happenings and the audio on the tablet. He told her about the search warrant and the investigation. Renee was confused, "I am beside myself, Carly. Who could have hurt Gwen and Why?" she asked, "Gwen was good, kind, loving, and loyal."

I agreed with Renee's assessment and consoled Renee, "She was a wonderful woman," I said. "Her death was a shock, and knowing it was not an accident adds another layer of grief and trauma for you and Shelby."

"Yes," Renee agreed as she wiped tears from her eyes.

"We will all need to help each other," George said as he left the terrace and gestured for me to look after Renee. Dalton called upstairs, "Renee has a call from Texas." She was just finishing a coffee with a smidge of Blackberry brandy. "I'll get to it, Carly." She left the terrace and turned back to me, "Carly, dear, I was a fortunate mother when my son married a fine and caring young woman. Why is it that the bad boys always get the good girls?" she asked. I watched her leave and hoped what she said was true. I was a good girl, wasn't I?

Chapter Twenty-Nine

It was a perfect day for a ride. I asked Shelby to have Raul saddle my bay. I started on the walking path to the barn. The sun was shining through the trees, creating warm spots of light that disrupted the coolness of the shade. I could see activity in and around the barn as horses for today's races were trailered for hauling. The pastures glistened, and the fall leaves were beautiful. I am a lucky woman, I thought. Despite the glaring mysteries of the Candiss Estate, life was good at this moment. My sins have not been realized, and my penance has not yet been handed down. Emotionally, I was wavering between what life was and what it could become. I was still waiting for the other shoe to drop and hoping it did not.

At the barn, it was all hands-on deck; it was bustling with activity. Tack was being gathered and stored in trailers, and horses were haltered and led out of their stalls, stable hands, jockeys, and Estate workers were given last minute instructions. Raul reminded the staff about the ongoing investigation and the need for cooperation. He encouraged staff with concerns to speak with George Candiss, who was eager to answer questions or provide guidance. Raul informed them of a pay raise and announced that all of the jockies would be paid as soon as payroll packets and tax forms were completed and turned in to Maxine. Raul was doing a good job replacing Michael in the role of Estate Personnel Foreman. It was not the time to talk with Raul, so I straddled my mount and ambled out to greet the day.

I let the bay have her head, and she ran happily and soundly through the Estate. We stopped along the North Garden path, and I treated her to two carrots and an apple which she sucked from my open palm and ate noisily. I walked her in the direction of the guest house and saw George's convertible and Maxine's Sedan parked in the back. I found myself wondering if they were in love or if it was a relationship based on convenience. I was sure Maxine's paycheck reflected her extra duties, as did George's attitude. Perhaps it was a win-win-win. Who was I to judge? I killed my husband and was having sex with a man and a woman. As I mounted my mare for the ride back, I saw a car approaching the guest house. I rode far enough away to be out of sight. I dismounted and watched the car. I recognized it . . . it was Judy's Mustang.

"What the hell?"

I tied my horse to the nearest tree and made my way on foot to the guest house. I ducked under the open window on the side nearest the front door.

Maxine, George, and Judy were sitting in the front room. Maxine served Judy a cup of hot coffee.

George said, "You understand the importance of this, Judy?"

"Yes," she said, "I do."

"When we hired Rosario, we couldn't have foreseen that he would kill Roger." George handed Judy an envelope, "This won't bring Roger back, but it will help you get started again. It will pay off Roger's gambling debt, so they won't come after you."

Judy said, "Thank you, Dad."

"And Carly mustn't know about this. Michael's cruelty, abuse, and infidelity were hard for Carly to bear, much less this . . ."

"I understand," Judy said.

I didn't know whether to ride away or burst in and demand to know the truth.

"DAD?" Did Judy call George, DAD? I heard Judy say, "Fran's parents are leaving town today."

George replied, "I wonder if we'll ever know who killed Fran? All we know is that Roger feared for your life, Judy."

She began to cry. Maxine handed Judy tissues and said, "Relationships are complicated in Merit – it's a small town – woven in a web of lies and deceit. Gambling is a vice, and the money always wins. Merit is hardly an appropriate name."

Judy agreed and tearfully said, "I'm worried about Carly. She's speaking with the FBI and asking questions."

George replied, "I'll watch out for Carly."

Judy nodded and stood to leave, "Thank you, Dad."

George and Judy hugged. I watched Judy drive away and I made my way to my mare.

I led the mare a good distance before mounting her. I was confused. My mind was spinning. DAD? Was Judy my sister-in-law? Who was her mother? "Wait a minute," I said out loud to Molly, "Judy's mom and dad are here in Merit now. Why was Judy calling George Dad?" I wondered who killed Fran? Was it a crime of passion? Was Rosario a jealous man or a paid assassin? Did

George pay off Roger's gambling debt to protect Judy? Why must it be a secret from me? What was George covering up? Did Shelby and Dalton know about Judy? Should I tell them what I saw and heard?

As I rode back to the barn, I remembered the gun boxes and wondered how they got into my closet. I thought about the guns registered to me and Michael. I was now convinced the boxes were placed there by Marc, but why was he setting me up for Roger's murder before Rosario spilled the beans? What information did George have that he wasn't sharing with the FBI? Where exactly was Marc now? Where did Michael fit in with all of this? Shelby told me in a moment of drunkenness to talk with Raul. What light could Raul shed on this unfolding drama? That's where I decided to start – with Raul, but when could I safely speak with him? And what was I missing about Maxine?

As I approached the barn, I was relieved to see Morty's car. He was in the stall with the colt, who was moving around well and already growing. I could see Morty was proud of his colt and somehow empowered. He met me and Molly at the barn doors.

"Darling," as he said, wrapped his hands around my waist, and lowered me to the ground. I handed the reins to Jim. Morty saw the look on my face. "Uh-oh," he said.

"Can I ask you something?"

"Of course, darling, anything."

I clarified, "It's about Judy."

"What about her?"

"Do you know where she was born?" I asked.

"Trevor, I think," he answered. "That's where her mom and dad live. She grew up there. Shelby would know. Judy and Shelby were together before Shelby met Gwen."

"Whoa, What? You never thought to mention that before?"

"No. Why would I? It wasn't a secret, and your friendship with Shelby is brand new, right?" I was blown away.

Morty drove me back to the house. Renee and all her staff were in the den. Renee was talking about the investigation and the necessity of providing fingerprints. "It's to rule out any of us as accessories and narrow the suspect list in Gwen's death. It's a requirement," she said.

"That's it, everyone, carry on." Shelby waved from across the room. Emily walked past and said dinner would be ready in an hour. Dalton left to put the limos in the garage, and Renee took my hand and asked, "How are you, dear?"

Shelby motioned to me to meet her upstairs, and I nodded in agreement.

"I am tired out, Renee. How about you?" I asked.

"Me too and feeling blue about Gwen and sad for Shelby," she said.

"I'm going to bed as soon as I eat. Emily has been working on a homemade turkey pie with vegetables from the garden. Good Southern Comfort food," she said.

"I can't wait."

I went upstairs. Shelby was waiting to steal a few moments away and tell me about the meeting with her Attorney and Gwen's life insurance.

"I saw Dr. Mortimer drop you off," she began.

"Yes, he did," I said. I hesitated and said, "Shelby, can I ask you about something?"

"Uh-oh," she said. "Such a serious tone."

"Were you and Judy a couple?"

Shelby blushed. "Carly, we were kids. That was 15 years ago. We were young. Gwen and I were together for twelve years between then and now. Why do you ask?"

"Why haven't you said anything about knowing Judy before?"

"What is this, Carly? Why does it matter?"

"Do you know who her parents are?" I asked.

"Her family moved to Trevor when we were in second grade. Her parents are Jeff and Marie Trudeau, from Texas."

"Where in Texas?" I questioned.

"Matrix," she said.

"The same town as the Candiss' trucking company."

Chapter Thirty

Bill Becker sat at the desk in George's office. The family was present. Maxine was there to record the reading of the will and address any necessary follow-up items or questions. George had arranged for a teleconference call for Joanne, who was in Texas. Renee was somewhat sober and had asked Dalton and Shelby to be there for her emotional and moral support. I sat between George and Renee. Renee squeezed my hand. Bill began by explaining the nature of the meeting. The first part of the will was a letter from Michael to his family, which Michael had requested that Bill read out loud to the group:

"To My Patronizing Family,

Insofar as I am far and away superior to any of you, I understand that you could never meet my need for validation. I know that my heightened awareness and inexplicable nature make it impossible for you to understand. Also, I must admit your understanding, as limited as it is, could never satisfy me. I appreciate you tried to love me, as much as I can appreciate any small act that could or would be of benefit. I am too far advanced to be appreciated by you. I am hated, loathed, ridiculed, and belittled. I live hard and intend to die hard, which, if you are reading this, I achieved. Bully for me. I am out -- and done with you. I write this for two reasons: 1) It is necessary for the state, and 2) To demonstrate I am capable of one kind act.

I leave everything I own to my wife, Carly Candiss, who suffered unrelenting abuse when the sole purpose was the reward of the abuse itself. Continuous abuse of the innocent gives one a sense of power that is addictive. It is a thirst that must be quenched. In return for the abuse, I leave all I have to Carly Candiss. As much as I can, I wish her well. I'm sure I have ruined her for any other man.

Joanne Seeger will keep a home in Texas or anywhere she chooses to live. Her home and monthly salary from the Candiss Corporation will be maintained for as long as she lives. I am sure my father will not dispute these requests. He must honor my wishes.

And I leave my love – if it is love at all – to the two most important people in my life: Renee, who loved me, as unconditionally as anyone ever could and to Raul who was my only true love. He was the reason I tried and failed for years to exile Dr. Mortimer. If I hadn't loved Raul as deeply as I was able, I would have killed the Doctor. So, to Raul, as a testament of my love for you, I leave the beloved Doctor and your job, but nothing more."

~Michael

The silence that crept into the room during the reading remained long after the letter was read. Renee and George stared blankly at one another. Maxine quietly fumed about George's mandate to provide for Joanne. Dalton and Shelby looked at one another and then at me. I realized that being awake, alert, and a part of -- had its downside. Bill Becker broke the silence, "Carly, come to my office next week, and we'll prepare the paperwork to transfer ownership of Michael's assets. Call the office and schedule something with my assistant. George, you'd better come too; this will have an impact on you." He snapped his briefcase closed and bid us a "Good afternoon."

I was now a wealthy woman who owned property in multiple states, several race horses, a piece of a trucking company in Texas, numerous deeds to real estate in Merit, Spencer, Cater, and Trevor, as well as all the land upon which were housed: The race track, adjoining work-out tracks, stables, and feed store. The county paid all the taxes on the land, for the rights to operate a "Gambling venue." I would receive a third of the profit during racing season and half of the profit for events in the off-season. The land was appraised at $13.2 million, with an additional annual revenue of $2.4 million. Suddenly, for the first time in my life, I had a bright future. I did not yet know what and who that future would include.

Shelby, Dalton, and I met in Shelby's quarters after George, Maxine, and Renee left to join Raul at the track. We discussed Renee and George and their response to the truth about Raul, Dr. Mortimer, and Michael. Renee and George were stoic at the reading. Emily showed up with beer and meat, fruit, and cheese trays. We filled her in on the reading. She was interested in Joanne's perks and their reasons. It wasn't long before our conversation returned to Gwen and her fall. I cautioned the group on sharing information with Maxine, "I realize that she's been a part of this family longer, but I would encourage you to speak wisely in front of her, trust me," I added. Everyone knew of Maxine's role and duties in terms of her job description, on and off the clock.

I made my way to my room and a much-needed afternoon nap. I fell into clean, white luxury sheets and drifted. As I lay there, I was grateful for all I had and was about to obtain. I thought of Morty's enmeshment with Raul -- and Michael's will-full disclosure. Did Morty know about Michael and Raul?

Of course, he did. Hence, the eagerness to rid this world of an evil man. Morty was really the winner here. He got what he wanted, but did I? I was rescued from a life of cruelty and abuse, but Morty and I would never be together; somehow, that made my crime more sinister and unforgivable. I was misled and perhaps manipulated again by a man who was supposed to love me.

My phone rang. It was Morty. I didn't answer. I heard the trailers coming back into the Estate from the track. I waited about an hour and walked to the barn. Raul was the only one left when I entered. He was filling out logs, and I startled him.

"Oh, Mrs. Candiss," he said, "I didn't see you there."

"I'm sorry, Raul. I didn't mean to scare you," I said.

"It's been a long day, Ma'am."

"How did our ponies do?" I asked.

"Overall, they did well. They need some work," he said. I walked into the stall where Morty and I had sex. Raul followed me with his gaze.

"I've made love to Morty in this stall," I said.

His smile turned to a frown. He said, "That's funny, Mrs. Candiss, so have I."

I looked into his eyes, "You and Morty are together for life, Raul?" I asked.

"Yes, ma'am, we are," he answered curtly. "And we are hoping you are more respectful than Michael," he snapped. I flushed. "Morty and I will be together long after his flirtations with other men and sexual interludes with women. We are meant to be," he said. I sensed his hold on Morty.

"I'm sorry, Raul," I said. "I misunderstood or was misled."

Raul nodded and sadly admitted, "That's not the first time I've heard that, ma'am, but trust me, we always end up together, even if it means eliminating those who come between us."

I gasped – took a long look at Raul – who glared at me. I left the barn. Tears leaped from my eyes as I closed the door behind me. I realized the terrible sin of which I had been a part. I was distraught. Had I been played?

"Oh, Morty," I said to the night.

Chapter Thirty-One

Jonah arrived at the barn on the Candiss Estate a little before noon. I was in Renee's office helping to finalize Gwen's Celebration of life, including an appearance by Carole King.

Renee said, "Honey, if money can't buy special favors to suit special needs, then money has no real value."

I had to agree. Shelby saw Jonah's SUV drive by the house and whispered, "Jonah's at the barn. Perhaps you'd like a walk."

I excused myself and left the final details to Renee and Shelby, who were much more suited for the task. As I closed the front door, I looked back at Shelby – her sorrow showed, but so did her love and respect for others.

"Mrs. Candiss," Jonah said happily. "You are a sight for these sore eyes." He was examining colt and mare.

"This young'un is doing well," he said. "As is his mother."

"That's good news, Jonah," I said half-heartedly.

"Why so down?" he asked.

"Gwen's life celebration is today," I said. "It is a hard day for Shelby – and she is a good friend."

"Yes," Jonah said, "but Gwen wanted a celebration, right? Let's celebrate Gwen's and Shelby's life together. They found something some folks never find."

His attitude made me smile. "But, it's more than that, Carly, isn't it?" he inquired. I felt a tear fall.

"Yes," I said, "but let's focus on joy in the friendships that come and go. Will you be there tonight?"

"With respectful bells on," he said. "Will you save me a dance?"

I agreed, "Thank you, Jonah."

As the evening approached, Shelby and I did our make-up. I tried to keep Shelby calm and focused.

She said, "I can't believe Renee got Carole King. I just can't believe it! Gwen would be elated."

I laughed, "She most-likely is! And I am beginning to understand that there is little Renee cannot accomplish."

"Oh, Carly, thank you for being kind and helpful and wonderful. I just can't imagine going through this without you."

"I wouldn't be anywhere else," I said.

Dalton called out to us and knocked, "Come in," we said.

He walked in with three glasses and Renee's special Cognac. He held up his glass and said, "I drink to my friends: Shelby, Gwen, and Carly."

We touched glasses and sipped the smooth elixir with a loud group, "AHHHH." Dalton turned on his heels and departed, "Ladies," he said on his way out.

"Shelby, have you seen Judy?" I inquired as I put on mascara and curled my eye lashes.

"She went away for a couple of weeks, I think," Shelby said as she applied a gloss over her ruby red lipstick.

"I heard that she is with her parents in Trevor. Haven't you talked to her?"

"I called, but no answer."

I stood to look in the full-length mirror. My red dress dropped just below my knees and fit tightly around my legs and hips, with a snug waist and a wrap-around swooping cowl.

"What do you think?" I asked.

Shelby looked up at me and gasped, "Oh, Carly, you are exquisite."

We both began to cry.

"Let's not ruin our make-up," I said.

She stood up and caressed me. She held me tightly but tenderly. It was her turn. She looked in the mirror. Shelby's dress was a backless, form-fitting, grey, purple, and teal that dropped to the floor. Her full breasts filled out the low-cut neckline, which accentuated a good amount of cleavage and a petite waist. Her eye shadow matched the colors in her dress and her eyes glowed blue. She was truly the most beautiful woman I had ever seen.

"Gwen would be proud," I said, "and jealous."

Shelby and I shared laughter, love, and sadness.

Carole King arrived with her band. Renee and George greeted them like royalty. Renee took me and Shelby by the hands and led us to Ms. King for introductions. We were like tearful teenagers. Carole offered condolences to Shelby and was personable and gracious. She autographed Gwen's bio and wrote a personal note: "The darkness of this loss is here and now -- but love lives on -- and the future will bring you together again in the light." Shelby was in tears and would remain that way, on and off, for the rest of the night. The guests began to gather, and the evening of respect for Gwen and support for Shelby began with Carole singing, "You've got a friend." There was not a dry eye in the house.

I saw Jonah come into the room. I looked around for other guests that I knew: Deena, from Fairchild's, was at the bar with her father. Oscar from the Waymark danced with Marlene from the track. Dalton was having a drink with Ellen from Pete's. Emily and Renee were having a snack with Ralph from the guard shack and Jim from the barn staff. George, Hector, and Mr. Hines were discussing tomorrow's races over cognac. I was surprised to see Starla Beam, but suddenly, it made sense when she scooped up Deena and twirled her around the dance floor to "Smackwater Jack." Many others I did not know were present and most-likely friends and/or business associates of Gwen and Shelby.

As the band started to play "So Far Away." Shelby tapped my shoulder, "May I have this dance?"

I felt myself blush as I stepped onto the dance floor. I cried softly as we held each other in a warm embrace. A tap on my shoulder, and Jonah gently turned me to face him as Oscar stepped in to dance with Shelby. When the song ended, the room was filled with enthusiastic applause. Everyone listened intently, and those on the dance floor held their positions and sang along to "Tapestry." This was the perfect celebration for Gwen. I saw Celia from the dress shop come in with Hattie from the coffee shop. I was filled with gratitude to finally be a part of something that felt authentic. I asked forgiveness from the universe for my crime and my sins. Morty and Raul did not attend. I was sure they had another perfect night together while everyone else was here.

Carole King began to sing the last song of the night -- the song Gwen wanted at her celebration. Shelby approached Jonah and I. She snuggled between us with her arms around each of our waists.

"Now and forever, you are a part of me, and the memory cuts like a knife

. . ." Shelby's face was wet with tears, "We had a moment," Carole sang – "just one moment . . ." Shelby buried her face in Jonah's jacket. "We are the lucky ones . . ." Shelby's knees grew weak and we supported her. Shelby's friends came over one by one and offered love and condolences. "Now and Forever, I will always be with you . . ."

Renee showed up with a tray of tequila shots. We all took one and drank to Gwen. Shelby indulged in several. I marveled at the support Shelby received, but I was especially touched by Jonah's kindness as he led Shelby to the dance floor for the encore song, "Way Over Yonder . . . that's where I'm bound."

As the night came to an end and I found Shelby and Carole King deep in conversation, I walked Jonah to the door.

"You are a good friend, Carly," he said, looking in Shelby's direction.

"Oh Jonah," I said, "I'm so happy to be awake and alive – I feel like I got my life back."

I dropped my eyes to the floor as I recalled how I got my life back. Guilt was a frequent companion and a high price to pay.

"Carly, life doesn't often give second chances. Please . . . take advantage."

Jonah wrapped his hands around my waist and pulled me close to him, "By the way, did I tell you of your utter beauty tonight?" Jonah kissed me gently.

"Goodnight," he said.

"Goodnight," I replied.

I felt the kiss linger on my lips.

Chapter Thirty-Two

The next morning came too soon for all of us. I had the second hangover of my life and woke in my room, accompanied by Celia and Shelby in my bed, Emily on the sofa by the terrace doors, and Starla and Deena wrapped in blankets on the floor. Everyone was asleep, and some were scantily clad. I tiptoed into the bathroom and turned on the shower. I thought about last night and what a wonderful celebration it was for Gwen and Shelby. I thought about Jonah, Morty, and Michael – the men in my life. Shelby appeared and stepped into the shower with me. She was unsteady and blurry-eyed as she wrapped her arms around me in a wet embrace.

"Wasn't last night perfect," she said.

"Perfect," I said as I hugged her and stepped out of the shower.

"Make room for me," Celia coughed out as she joined Shelby under the warm water.

I slipped into my robe and smiled as life took another kind turn.

I towel-dried in front of the mirror and watched the reflection of Celia and Shelby taking turns soaping each other's backs. I was taken with the wonderful normalcy of life in fleeting moments. I stepped into my room to find Emily still asleep and Starla and Deena lying awake, laughing about last night's visit with Carole King. I opened the terrace doors and was surprised to find Oscar and Marlene cuddled together on the Terrace. "Good morning," Oscar said. Marlene rolled over, and she and Oscar went back to sleep. "That was some party," I said out loud.

The air coming from the terrace was fresh and cool. I heard the vehicles loading for the track and the horses whinny as they were loaded. I smelled the wood burning in the fireplaces and knew that Dalton was holding down the fort for everyone else this morning. I wondered how Renee was. The last thing I remembered was Renee dancing with Jim to a karaoke version of Cracklin' Rosie after the band left. She drank a lot of tequila. I saw Maxine and George get her up to bed and then leave by the back door. Like father like son, they never got enough.

Renee called upstairs. "Have you seen Emily?" she asked.

"I have a dreadful headache and George wants his eggs."

"She is here," I said. "I'll send her down."

"Thank you, Carly, I need her," she said.

I went to the sofa and shook Emily. "Wake up, Emily," I said. "George wants his eggs."

Emily opened one eye and looked at me in bewilderment. "Where am I?" she asked.

We all laughed as Emily sat up and disclosed her dream about being on a deserted island with Carole King's drummer. I was sorry I woke her. She scrambled to her feet and out the door in a haze.

I opened the door to my closet and was surprised to see eight large boxes from Elite Clothing.

"Oh, Shelby," I called out – "look what's here." Shelby appeared wrapped in a towel. Celia followed, and Deena and Starla came in, too.

"Well, ladies, shall we," I said -- and we all opened a box. We went through the clothing, from boots to bras and dresses to dungarees.

"You have great taste," Celia said.

"Thank you, coming from you, that's a compliment," I replied.

"Oh, Carly, can I try this on?" Deena asked.

"Of course." Shelby opened a box and said, "These are the two dresses you ordered for me."

"Perfect," I said. "Try them on."

Starla was happy just to watch these beautiful women in various stages of undress.

"This is my kind of morning," she said, and we all laughed. I had friends with whom I was comfortable and for whom I cared. I realized I truly was a wealthy woman.

After the guests left, I found Renee in the office. She had several Bloody Marys and was feeling fine. She was encouraged by the turnout and support last evening. Carole King was now her favorite entertainer of all time. She noted that Raul and Dr. Mortimer were not in attendance.

"Men who love men, Carly. I don't understand. Maybe it's like Michael said. I'm not capable."

"That's not true, Renee. You are capable," I said. "You are too loving to judge or label."

"I guess so," she said with a sigh, "and I try not to worry over trifles."

Shelby came in carrying a tray of biscuits, eggs, potatoes, bacon, and ham, followed by Emily with a pot of coffee. They set the trays down and started out of the office when Renee called after them.

"Sit down, ladies," she said. "Join us for breakfast."

Shelby and Emily were surprised and timidly joined us. Renee poured the coffee. I realized Renee was as lonely with George as I was with Michael. It is a harsh reality when a woman realizes the absence of love and intimacy -- from the man to whom she is married. I felt her pain and the importance of this breakfast together.

The phone rang. Renee answered. "OH? She said, "I'll call him right away, Doctor. Yes, I'll tell her." Renee hung up. "That was Jonah," she said. "Your presence is requested at the barn. It's about Miss Molly."

I jumped out of my chair and ran toward the barn.

"I'll call George," Renee called after me. I was out of breath when I reached the barn. Jonah was in the stall with Miss Molly, who was lying down in the straw. I gasped, "What is it, Jonah?"

"I'm not sure yet, Carly."

"How long has she been down?" I asked.

"The stable hand called me at 4:30 and I came right away."

"Oh Jonah, no!" I cried.

Miss Molly tried to raise her head. "She is responding to you, Carly," Jonah said. "Try to get her to stand."

I chirped her name and clicked my cheek like always. She lifted her head but did not stand. I pulled at her halter. She was able to get her front legs under her but could not lift herself from a lying position. George came into the barn. He was freshly shaven and showered. He looked concerned.

Jonah stepped toward George and shook his hand. George touched my back and said, "Hello, dear." He and Jonah left the stall. I felt the ominous indication of them talking outside. I joined them. Jonah said, "I drew blood. We'll get the results back this afternoon. She is weak, but I am hydrating her. She is a strong mare, in good shape. This may be the virus that went around the track last week. She could have been exposed by one of the other horses. Any of them sick, George?" Jonah asked.

"Not that I know of," George said. "But some of Mitch Malcom's horses were hit last week. We ponied with them." I went back into the stall with my girl. "This is just a virus, Molly. It will pass, I promise. Be strong."

I heard George drive away. Jonah rejoined me. "Carly, I'm going to give her an anti-viral before I get the test results. I feel like we shouldn't wait."

"Of course," I said, "whatever you think."

Jonah stepped out to call his office, and I began to weep. He returned and took me firmly in his arms. I felt it all wash over me; everything hit me at once. I sobbed into Jonah's sweatshirt until it was soaked from my tears. When I drew back from him, I was looking into the eyes of a man who loves me. His gaze was compassionate and piercing. He kissed me, and I kissed him back. He kissed me again, longer and deeper. We drew away from each other and there was Dr. Mortimer, standing in the barn door.

Morty stepped back, "I thought I might be of assistance. I see I was wrong."

He abruptly exited the barn. I started after him, but Jonah held on to my arm.

"Do you really want to go, Carly?" he asked.

No, I didn't.

Chapter Thirty-Three

Weeks passed. Molly recovered after hydration and antivirals. Bill Becker and I completed the paperwork for the process of reassigning Michael's assets. I sold two geldings to Mitch Malcolm and one mare to Starla. Renee and I talked about my move from the Estate, but I had not yet decided where to go. Renee was in no hurry to see me leave. We had grown to love one another. Morty came to the main house less. His time on the Estate was mostly spent at the barn, and he kept his visits brief. Jonah and I were what Shelby called "an item." It felt good to love a man who loved me. I bore the burden of my sins quietly. I hoped to one day be free of guilt, but underneath it all, I felt I would and should be punished for the grave offense of Michael's murder.

Renee changed the schedules for all her staff. Each member now had one day off per week and a raise in pay. She hired another cook. Emily became the supervisor of the kitchen and replaced Gwen as Renee's personal assistant. Dalton was now in charge of all transportation in and out of the Estate, and another driver was hired to replace Marc. Shelby hired a plane and Spread Gwen's ashes over East Lake. I was no longer experiencing memory lapses and received a clean bill of health from Dr. Nadal. Michael's clothing and personal belongings were donated to St. Mark's ministry for the elderly in Merit, and things on the Estate seemed routine and "normal." The investigation into Gwen's death resulted in a change of cause from an accidental death to a homicide. Everyone on the Estate was cleared of wrongdoing, and Marc, who was now AWOL from Candiss Enterprises, was considered more than a "Person of interest."

Shelby and I went to Hattie's for an espresso and ran into Starla. She bounced over and squeezed us in her usual raucous fashion.

"Congratulations," she said as she pushed her fist into my shoulder. "It's about time someone landed that horse doctor."

Shelby laughed, and Starla said, "Too bad she couldn't have nabbed one of us."

We all laughed.

Shelby winked at Starla and said, "Yeah, our team couldn't snag her, but we tried." Starla left the shop laughing. "I AM happy for you, Carly," Shelby said, "and I want you to know my only regret is that Gwen didn't get the chance to know you."

Shelby and I walked down the street with our coffee. We walked by Judy's shop. It was boarded up, and there was a sign that said, "Closed for remodeling."

"Shelby, let's not go back to the Estate. Let's drive to Trevor."

Shelby asked, "Why in the world . . .?"

I interrupted her, "Shelby, I need to tell you something."

"I'm all ears," she said, surprised by my sudden change in tone.

"Do you remember the day I asked you about your relationship with Judy?" I asked.

"Yes, how could I forget?"

"Well, I overheard Maxine, George, and Judy at the guest house on the North End."

"What?" Shelby said in disbelief.

"Yes. George handed Judy an envelope of money to pay off Roger's gambling debt," I said.

"Now, who is keeping secrets?" Shelby blurted out.

"Sorry," I said. "I was uncertain about who to trust."

"There's more," I said. "Brace yourself, and you must not say a word to anyone, promise?" Shelby made a gulping sound.

"Yes, I promise, but is it something you're sure you want to tell me?" she asked.

I whispered, "Judy called George DAD!"

Shelby Squealed in disbelief. "Carly, what have you been drinking . . . Why?"

"How about we drive to Trevor and talk to Judy – we are all old friends. She might need our help. Something doesn't make sense. She might have insight into Gwen's death, who tried to frame me, and who tried to drain my accounts dressed as me and Michael. What do you think?"

We gassed up my Camry, bought some White Cheddar popcorn, and left for Trevor.

"God only knows what we'll find out, Shelby. Are you sure you want to go?"

"Hell yes!" she said.

On the drive over, Shelby and I processed all the information we had. We speculated about ideas and outcomes. We tried to see angles and how others could be harmed or prosper from what we knew. It was Shelby who wondered, "If George is Judy's dad, could Joanne then be Judy's mother?" We recalled the remark in Michael's will about Joanne keeping her job and home and – to that end -- George's obligation. It may explain the secrecy around Joanne and Marc, but where does Judy fit in? I said, "Judy is 32, and if Joanne gave birth at 14, that would make Joanne 46. Mathematically, it works out. How did this tie into Roger and Fran's death, or did it? What about Gwen? We were anxious to speak with Judy. Shelby tried Judy's number again. Still -- there was no answer."

My phone rang. It was Jonah. I was driving. "Let it go to voicemail," I said.

"Carly, are you happy?" Shelby asked.

"I almost hate to admit it, Shelby, but I am. The chaos around Michael was too much for me, and I do love Jonah. I miss Morty. He was someone special, who I trusted. He betrayed that trust; he misled me."

"How so?" Shelby asked.

"Well, I can't say. You'll have to believe me about that."

"OK," she said.

"I believe you. You know, Carly, some things are better left unsaid."

I agreed and added, "Like Renee says, let's not worry over trifles."

Shelby said with melancholy, "Well, at least you give me hope that I can love again."

Quiet fell over us; we turned up the radio.

In a few minutes, we would reach Trevor.

Chapter Thirty-Four

The town of Trevor was bigger than Merit. Trevor was rumored to be more progressive. The town itself was condensed with new apartment complexes and two multiple-level condominium communities with roof gardens and gated entrances. The outlying suburban area was developing and included a grocery store chain, small strip malls, restaurants, bowling alleys, and plenty of daycare. There was a widespread rural area that provided fresh local produce, as well as pork, beef, chicken, turkey, and eggs. The weekend farmer's market did well in Trevor. A new 24-hour cyber network facility came to town approximately two years ago and brought with it 2,000 jobs, hence Trevor's expansive growth and "progressive" label.

I called Judy's cell. She did not answer. I was beginning to worry. We parked in the center of town, across from the bowling alley on Main Street and adjacent to the entrance, outside a circle drive for the mall. I asked Shelby if she knew where Judy's mom's shop was. She did not. We googled it and found that we were on the wrong side of the square. Shelby said, "Nice day for a walk," and we followed the blue dot on our GPS. The town was clean. New shops were springing up on every block. The landscaping was exquisite, with colorful flowers lining the walkways. The courts and quads were green with well-maintained topiaries.

"You have arrived," our GPS informed us, but there was no salon at the location. We walked down a few doors, and then back the other way, still no salon. There was a small Ice Cream Parlor, an Adidas shoe store, and a Sporting Goods Store. There was one empty storefront, boarded up on the end closest to the street, but no indication what it was or would be. Shelby and I shrugged at each other. She asked if I felt like having ice cream. "More than I need a pair of Adidas," I answered. We ordered our usual Jamoca Almond Fudge and Chocolate Mint.

"Do you know where we can find Marie's Hair Affair?" I asked.

The young man behind the counter shook his head, "Nah."

We took our ice cream into the sporting goods store. We found several young male employees with earbuds who had "no idea" about the salon. They pointed to the barbershop across the street, who would give us a good deal if we mentioned them by name. Shelby spotted an older woman exiting the back door and made a beeline for her.

"Excuse me, ma'am," she said. "Can you direct us to 'Marie's Hair Affair?"

"Nope," she said, "it doesn't exist."

Shelby showed the woman the GPS.

"Yeah, it did exist until about a week ago. Then Marie's daughter came to town, and within a week, Marie, her husband, her daughter, the horse, and the family dog moved to Texas."

I asked, "Do you know where in Texas?"

"Nope," she said. "I told you all I know."

"We drove a long way for an ice cream cone," Shelby said.

Back in the car, Shelby and I were perplexed. We'd known Judy for years. She was a good friend, well-known and well-liked in Merit. I started to wonder what all of this meant in terms of Michael. Was Joanne Judy's mother, and George -- Judy's dad? Did that make my late husband Judy's half-brother? She hated Michael – maybe there was more to it than we were aware. Perhaps she had reasons of her own to loathe Michael. But then, why was he "keeping" Joanne? Was Joanne his mistress, as everyone assumed – or his mother? What about Renee? She was Michael's only ally – but wait . . . Joanne was deeply bereaved at his funeral. Who could tell me more; how could I find out? I started the car, and we decided to visit Merit County's Bureau of Vital Statistics. I had a nagging feeling I should ask Renee . . .

Chapter Thirty-Five

"I'll look for Marie and Jeff's marriage Certificate," Shelby said.

"You may as well look for George and Renee's, too, while you're in those files," I suggested and added, "I'll look for Judy and Michael's birth certificates. We each paid our $4.00 fee and received a password to use the database. I began my search for Judy Trudeau and entered Judy's birthdate 04-26-1990. Nothing. I searched for Judy Candiss. Nothing again. I searched for Judy/no last name, same birthdate, and got a hit." Judy Seeger, birth mother Joanne Seeger; birth father unknown. There was an addendum: Sealed adoption. I couldn't wait to tell Shelby. I continued my search. I entered Michael Candiss and his birthdate. Nothing. I entered Michael Seeger. Bingo! Birth mother Joanne Seeger; father unknown, with an addendum: Sealed adoption.

Shelby appeared. "I have good news and bad news," she said.

"Give me the bad news," I sighed.

"Well, there is no marriage certificate for Marie and Jeff Trudeau. That makes sense if they were married in another county and state. The good news is there is a marriage certificate for George and Renee who were married in 1978, here in Merit County. What did you find?" she asked.

"Well, brace yourself," I said, and I told her what I found.

Shelby gasped, "Whaaaat?" she squealed out loud, "I can't believe it."

"Joanne isn't Michael's mistress at all. Joanne is Michael's mother," I said.

"Carly, Joanne would have been about fourteen when Judy was born.

"Oh my God," I said. "The apple truly doesn't fall far from the tree." I must talk to Renee, but how could I ever bring this up?

We started the drive back to the Estate when Shelby said, "Carly – Marc and Joanne are siblings, right? Joanne was a young teen when she gave birth to Judy and Michael. Do you suppose that Marc and Joanne were gainfully employed with the Candiss Corporation as some kind of hush agreement? I nodded, "I feel like I'm living in a soap opera."

Shelby replied, "Welcome to my world, honey."

We laughed and dispelled some stress and suspicion. Shelby put in Carole

King's CD, and we sang to one another all the way back to Merit.

When we arrived back at the Estate, I asked Shelby to walk with me to the barn.

"Ok, but It's going to rain," she said.

I was still thinking about all we had learned.

"Shelby, what if Gwen, in her administrative role with Renee, stumbled upon some damaging information? Would Marc want to silence her, or at least get the tablet? Perhaps Gwen's fall was an accident in the struggle over the computer?"

"Gwen would have said something, Carly. She did not keep secrets from me." "What if she had just found out," I asked.

"I suppose so," Shelby said, "but what could she have seen that wasn't already known to those involved?"

"Good point," I agreed. But something gnawed at me. "Shelby, What do we know about Marc?"

She thought for a long minute and replied, "Nothing, Carly, outside the obvious – his employment with George and his family ties with Joanne."

"That's where we need to start," I said.

"You ask Dalton, Raul, and Jim. I'll ask Morty, Emily, and Ralph, OK? Then, we'll compare notes." We agreed to the plan as we entered the barn. Raul was in the stall with the stud.

He greeted us, "Ladies."

"Hello, Raul," Shelby said. I nodded, and he tipped his hat. "What can I do for you?" The stud had his ears pinned back and was stomping one of his front hooves in the straw. Raul soothed the stud. "Whoa boy, whoa boy, easy now. Studs don't like sharing space," Raul said as he climbed out of the stall. "Neither do mares," I replied. I couldn't help myself. Shelby shot me a glance that said, "Shut up!" I left the barn.

I walked to the guard shack at the back gate. The skies looked ominous. Ralph was on duty.

"Mrs. Candiss," he said happily, "This is a nice surprise."

"Hi Ralph," I said. "Can I ask you something?"

"Sure thing, ma'am."

"What can you tell me about Marc?"

Ralph looked surprised, "Well, ma'am, he drove for Mr. C for more than ten years. Marc was in prison before that. He recently went to work for Mr. Candiss in Texas but is AWOL now."

"Ralph, why was he in prison?"

"Don't know ma'am. Just hearsay," he said.

"And what did the hearsay suggest?"

Ralph took a breath, "Well, ma'am, I don't like to spread rumors, but I think he was in prison for rape. Some say, he took the fall for another fella."

"Thank you," Ralph. Could we keep this between us?"

"Yes, ma'am, if you don't walk out this gate, I don't have to record anything."

"Thank you," I said and walked back toward the barn.

I saw Shelby walking away and called out to her.

"What did you find out?" I asked.

Shelby was excited, "Marc has disappeared. Apparently, Jeff Trudeau has taken over Marc's duties in Matrix, and Judy and Marie are opening a salon there in about a month. They left town due to the mystery surrounding Roger's death and possible danger to the family. The FBI is involved with their protection. Raul said Marc was in prison before he came to work for Mr. Candiss, but he didn't know why. And another thing – Joanne has moved off the Candiss property. She is living in Greely. Raul told me that since Michael's death, Joanne wanted nothing else to do with the Candiss family."

"Wow," I said, "Anything else?"

"Well, yes," she said timidly, "Raul said Morty is miserable without you."

I was surprised by the tears as they spilled from my eyes. Shelby gently reached over and wiped them with her soft and supportive hands.

"His choices, his consequences," I replied mournfully.

"What did you find out?" Shelby asked.

"Pretty much the same," I said. I told her what matched her version from

Raul and added, "Ralph wasn't sure why Marc was in prison but heard that Marc took the fall for someone on a rape charge." Shelby's jaw dropped. "I know," I said. "Did George Candiss rape Joanne when she was 13, or did the pregnancy reveal an older man having consensual sex with a minor? Which by any account is illegal and would have ruined George."

We arrived at the Estate, and Shelby suggested that we invite Dalton and Emily down to Shelby's quarters for wine and conversation. Shelby would arrange it, and I would join them after a shower and a change into my sweats. As the warm water bathed me with new energy, my mind was racing. Where was Marc now? Was he fleeing the law? Was he, at one time, the sacrificial lamb for George? Were Michael and Judy the result of rape, infidelity, or products of George's love for a young woman other than the woman he married? I had a new, heartfelt compassion for Renee. I was beginning to realize why Judy hated Michael. He abused the privilege that Judy never had. He used that privilege to secure an impressive status and standing in the community, which he used to perpetuate hate and unfairness.

Emily and Shelby had finished their first glass of wine when I arrived. Thunder cracked, and the wind blew hard against the shutters. Dalton was just opening his second beer. I asked him to open one for me. Shelby and I brought them up to date. Dalton took in the information we relayed. He added that Mr. Candiss had known Marc since he was a boy in Matrix.

Dalton said, "Marc shined shoes at the airport and soon became a Texas errand boy for Mr. C. When Marc was old enough, he became the limo driver. Emily sat quietly.

"What do you think, Emily?" I asked. She said that Renee was more inebriated than usual one night, and she shared something interesting.

Renee cautioned Emily, "You must never worry over trifles. Some people are betrayers; it's their nature. I hope George figures it out before it is too late."

We all stared blankly at one another. We were perplexed. Emily gauged our responses.

Chapter Thirty-Six

After a couple more drinks, we all called it a night. I went up to my suite and settled into bed. A few short minutes later, I heard the door open, and Shelby said softly, "Carly, can I sleep in here?" I rolled toward the door and folded down the covers on the other side of the bed. Shelby shuffled in and snugged her back against my back. "Thank you," she said. It felt nice to have her close.

"You're welcome," I said.

We quickly drifted off to sleep as the winds picked up and rain began to fall.

The storm whipped up winds and dropped hard rains. Lightning ripped across the sky, and thunder cracked loudly above the Estate. There would be no races in Merit tomorrow. All hands would be in the barn and monitoring corrals to look after the stock through the night. The storm was loud and somewhat disturbing. Shelby awoke and rolled over. She put her arm over my waist and pulled closer to me. I felt more secure, but I felt something more. I felt a warm sensation run through my body. I know Shelby felt it, too. I thought of Jonah and Gwen. Would they mind?

I rolled over, facing Shelby. I kissed her warmly, softly. She was looking into my eyes. She had a tender smile on her face.

I said, "Shelby, I am not gay."

"I know," she answered as she kissed me again.

I understood Gwen's love and appreciation for Shelby. She was a wonderful woman and a good friend. Shelby fell deeply asleep. I lay awake and thought about judgement. I had judged myself and others, harshly. I was wrong. It seems, I was wrong about many things. It was dawning on me that others' wanted Michael dead and I was as much a dupe as an accomplice. I drifted to sleep, enlightened, relaxed and satisfied, no longer remorseful.

When morning found us, Shelby popped out of bed. "Ooh, I'm late," she said. She threw on her robe and ran out. I rolled over.

"Another hour," I mumbled. But the sandman left with Shelby, and I could not go back to sleep. I wanted to talk to Jonah and Morty to see what they knew about Marc. I was curious about Mr. Hines: Why his bodyguard duty ended and what he knew about Marc. I would ask him to pay me a visit? I wondered why Judy had not reached out. What was going on that kept her from answering our calls? A big part of me wanted to talk to Renee and pick her brain. Maybe it was time for another luncheon at the Waymark and a few cocktails, too many.

Shelby came in with coffee and hot pastries. I sat up in bed. She buttered a croissant, added cream to the coffee, and put the tray over my lap.

I told her about my plan to take Renee to lunch and begged her to get herself invited. We agreed and I would talk to Renee after breakfast. Shelby said that Mr. C was "in a mood" and she'd better get to work.

She told me, "The new cook woke up late this morning, and Mr. C's eggs were late. He grumbled that he was tired of everyone's slacking off since Michael's death."

I found Renee out front, in muddy rain boots, pruning roses. She was in a particularly good mood, as she often was when Mr. C was out of sorts.

I greeted her from the porch.

"Good morning, Renee," I said.

"Carly, dear, look at these roses; aren't they wonderful? They enjoyed the rain."

"Beautiful," I said.

"They are small individual works of art," Renee observed. "Don't you think so?"

"Yes," I agreed, "They are gifts from the earth to the deserving."

Renee smiled, "I like that."

"Renee," I said, "Let's go to the Waymark for lunch. We need a break, a good meal, and a few drinks."

"Oh Carly, that sounds delightful; my treat, and ask Shelby, too. I'll meet you back here at 12:30. I must change and get out of these dreadful boots."

Chapter Thirty-Seven

Dalton drove us to the Waymark. The streets were wet from the rain and empty due to the track's closure. The clouds still hung low overhead. It was cold. We all had on long pants and jackets, and Shelby wore a black leather vest with a matching "newsboy hat" that looked precious on her. The restaurant smelled delicious. Oscar met us at the door, "Ladies, you are in luck – special seafood gumbo prepared by our chef today. Freshly made and served hot with homemade golden brown biscuits."

"Say no more," Renee demanded. "Bring us three bowls of gumbo and a bottle of your best red."

The wine was served as we shed our jackets and settled into our seats. The gumbo was delivered piping hot and exquisite with the warm rolls and honey. A second bottle of wine arrived.

Renee ordered another gumbo and said, "It is just like mama made."

Oscar came to the table with a dessert menu – "Ladies, another special the Chef has been working on all morning: Cream cheese, lemon mousse; his own recipe. You've never had this before -- goes very well with cognac," he advised and winked as he walked away.

Renee said gleefully, "Oh girls, let's try that, too."

As she finished her second bowl of gumbo, she ordered three cream cheese lemon mousse and three cognacs. Oscar was right; we never had anything like it, and it went so well with the cognac that we ordered another.

Shelby was the first to speak up. She said, "I wanted to thank you, Renee, for everything you did for me and Gwen, especially for the support when Gwen died." Tears welled up in our eyes.

Renee replied, "Nonsense, Shelby – no need to thank me – we are family. Gwen was like a daughter to me."

I thanked Renee for her help and support, as well. "You have been a good friend, Renee," I said.

Renee put her hand up in the air as if to stop me from speaking, "Carly, you saved my son. You were the one good thing he had in his life. He didn't deserve you."

I felt a huge pang of guilt. Shelby asked, "Have things been ok between you and Mr. C? We've noticed some tension."

Renee motioned for Oscar to bring the check. Shelby and I offered to pay, but Renee insisted. She said, "This is a conversation for another venue."

She paid the bill, and we all walked out. Renee was staggering slightly. Shelby and I took an arm each and walked beside her. Renee made a grand exit, waving to the staff and hugging the busboys. She gave Oscar a hundred dollars and reminded him to share.

"Dalton, Let's go to the Backwater Bar," Renee shouted. "I am going to ride that mechanical bull if it kills me."

Dalton asked, "Are you sure, ma'am?"

"I am," Renee announced, and we drove away laughing.

In the limo, Renee lamented about Michael's sudden death, the loss of Gwen, and guilt about Roger.

"I should have helped with his gambling debt. He was a nice boy. I held a grudge because I was purposefully and completely kept out of Judy's life. Plain and simple, I held a grudge. It might have made a difference for Michael to have a sister. Instead, he grew up in a home divided by resentment, jealousy, and betrayal. Division was always Joanne's plan. You don't know what I'm talking about, but trust me, Secrets killed Michael, Roger, and Gwen. Now, secrets will kill Marc. George ruined Marc's life long ago, just like he ruined Michael's, Joanne's, and . . . perhaps mine. I blame George first -- for his sins in Texas -- and Joanne second. She was a child then but has long since grown up."

Shelby, Dalton, and I listened intently but did not say a word. The cognac proved to be truth serum.

"We're here, ma'am," Dalton said.

"Let's ride that bull," Renee cheered.

Inside the Backwater, it was dark and dank. It smelled like beer, sawdust, and Polish sausage. The locals were mostly seated at the bar, which ran the length of the room. Many of them were regulars at the racetrack. The jukebox was playing Dolly Parton. The mechanical bull hung still and silent. It was surrounded by black, bulky fall pads in the middle of what was the dance floor on weekends. I had never visited this establishment and was surprised that Renee had. Shelby and I looked wide-eyed at each other and smiled.

The owner, Jack Renner, was barely visible behind the bar. He howled like a coyote when he saw Renee, "If it isn't Renee Chamboree." Renee tap-danced to the bar, and she and Jack dosey-doed across the floor. Renee's smile was as wide as the bar was long. Renee gestured to us to come over.

She said, "Jack, these are my people."

He shook our hands, "Delighted to see you. He winked at Dalton. Any friend of Renee's is a friend of mine."

Renee ordered a pitcher of beer and told Jack to "Fire up that bull." Renee gave Dalton a ten-dollar bill and said, "Play every Carole King song." Jack turned on the bull and sat at the levers. Renee kicked off her shoes and jacket and said, "Giddy-up," as she mounted the black metal menace waiting to be ridden.

"Be careful, Renee," I cautioned.

Shelby yelled, "Good luck, Renee, hold on tight."

Dalton said, "Do not hurt yourself."

Jack was an expert at the controls. He moved the bull in a slow, bucking motion. He increased the speed slightly. Renee sat with her hips forward, heels dug in, shoulders back, and one hand waving high over her head. She squealed, "Yee-haw." Jack increased the speed slightly, and the bull moved to the right while bucking, then to the left, to the right, and up and down. Jack increased the speed and the movements. Renee held on until she began laughing too hard; the bull overtook her and threw her to the mat. Shelby and I ran out to Renee, but she came up laughing harder than I had ever seen her laugh. Jack was laughing, too.

"It brings back memories, doesn't it," he said, "Next?"

Dalton, Shelby, and I took turns on the bull. Dalton had the best ride and had the roughest workout with Jack at the controls. He was easy on Shelby and me since we were "greenhorns." We had a great time but did not get more information from Renee. She passed out on the way home after repeating, "YIPPEE-KYY-YAY."

Dalton said, "I would take Renee there to meet Michael on bad days at the track. Renee and Jack knew each other in high school. She probably would have married Jack if Mr. C hadn't promised her the moon. Jack was a jockey back then. He knows a lot about horses. He was injured at Merit Downs when the starting gate malfunctioned and backed over him. He sued and bought the bar with the settlement. "I was transfixed on the multi-dimensional layers of life. There is so much to know and learn."

I was awakened from my trance by the phone. It was Jonah.

"Hello," I said.

Jonah was his usual pleasant self. "Hi, love," he said. "Care to ride with me tomorrow? I've cleared my schedule. Molly is a mudder, isn't she?"

I laughed, "Sure," I said. "Sounds good, but do I have to wait till tomorrow to see you?"

"I like the sound of that," he answered. "Should I come by this evening?"

I glanced up and saw Shelby smiling at me. "Yes," I said. "Please do. We are on our way to the Estate and should be there in twenty minutes. Can you give me an hour?"

"Oh, and by the way, we've been drinking all afternoon."

"Really," Jonah laughed. "I'd better catch up. I'll see you soon, Carly. Love you," he said as he hung up.

Shelby mouthed, "I love you, too."

I closed my eyes and rested for the remainder of the trip. Life is so interesting.

Chapter Thirty-Eight

It was just after eight when Jonah rang the doorbell at the Estate. Dalton had started a fire in the den's gas fireplace and left for the garage to tuck in the limos. I told Shelby to take the night off after we secured Renee in bed. The ever-vigilant Emily and the new kitchen help were finishing up in the dining room and discussing tomorrow's menu and mealtimes. I had changed into a colorful and comfortable low-cut, wrap-around house dress that flowed to the floor. Jonah and I went into the den and I poured us a Benedictine Brandy in small snifters.

We sat on the sofa facing the fire, and Jonah raised his glass, "To the most beautiful woman I have ever seen. I am a lucky man."

I blushed and believed Jonah's sincerity. I was warm and happy.

"What do you know about Marc?" I asked.

Jonah was surprised by the question. "I don't really know Marc," he said. "I mean, other than knowing he was George's driver, Maxine's good friend, and Joanne's brother . . ."

I sensed Jonah's unwillingness to spend our time talking about Marc. I put my feet in Jonah's lap and changed the subject. He gently rubbed my feet as we discussed my move from the Estate. He recommended I use his realtor to look at some properties in Merit proper. He said there were some nice properties close to the track but far enough away not to be disturbed by noise or traffic. I would be closer to his place and his office, as well.

"I hadn't thought about buying anything," I said.

"I own enough real estate."

"Yes, Carly, but where do you want to live?"

I had not thought about it since the move to Vermont ended with Morty. Where did I want to live?

Between the foot rub, the fire, and the amount of liquor I consumed during the day, I was forced to say goodnight to Jonah at around ten. I walked him to the door, and he kissed me gently.

He said, "Good night, beautiful. I'll see you at what? 11:00ish for our ride?"

"That sounds wonderful," I said. "I'll be ready; just meet me at the barn."

We kissed again, and Jonah left. I made it halfway upstairs when I turned around and headed to the basement. I knocked and opened the door. Shelby was in bed, staring at the TV.

"Come in, Carly. What's up?" she asked.

I began to weep. Shelby pulled the covers down, and I crawled in next to her. She covered me, and we fell asleep in each other's arms.

"Thwap, Thwap, Thwap – Crash!"

We were awakened by loud noises and ran upstairs. Renee screamed as she fought back. "Thwap," Marc struck her again. Renee rolled downstairs with blood coming from her head. I screamed. Marc ran out the front door and sped away. Shelby ran to Renee. I called 911 and then Raul's cell. He picked up with a sleepy voice.

"Raul, Marc just assaulted Renee and is heading your way in Mr. C's convertible."

"What the hell?" Raul replied. "I bet he's looking for George and Maxine," he said. "I'd better warn them." He hung up. I called Morty and told him about Renee and my call to 911. He would meet the ambulance at the hospital.

Raul called George's cell phone. George answered angrily and breathlessly, "What?"

"Marc assaulted Renee and is heading your way," Raul declared. "Shit. Let the guards know. Tell them to stop Marc -- and Raul, -- call the police."

George pulled on his pants and shouted to Maxine, "Get up! Take my gun and get in the closet."

"What is it, George?" Maxine asked in a terrified tone.

"It's Marc. He's off the rails. He just assaulted Renee. He's on his way here."

Maxine called Marc's cell.

"Hello!" Mark shouted. "Where are you bitch?" Marc slurred angrily.

"Have you been drinking?" she asked.

"Shut up." He snapped. "Are you with him? I'm coming, and I'll kill you both," Marc said and tossed the phone out the car window.

Renee was groaning. Emily stabilized Renee's neck with a sash from the curtains, elevated her head on two pillows from the couch, and wrapped her in a blanket. Emily suggested all employees in the main house stay together. We log-rolled Renee onto a rug and dragged her into George's office. Shelby and the kitchen staff tended to Renee. Emily and I moved the couch against the locked door. Emily blocked the bathroom door by tipping a filing cabinet onto an overstuffed chair in case Marc tried to return through the bathroom window. We all hid on the floor behind George's desk. Emily was resourceful in a crisis. Grateful for her wherewithal, I gave her an enthusiastic thumbs up. We heard sirens entering the property through the front gate and gunshots coming from the back of the estate. Renee wailed.

The commotion ended as quickly as it began. We all listened. We heard engines coming and going but nothing else. We did not dare leave the office. A loud knock on the door startled us.

I called out, "Who is it?"

Raul answered, "It's me, Carly, and Mr. Hines."

Emily and I moved the couch. I unlocked the door.

"Where's Renee?" Mr. Hines asked.

I motioned toward the desk, and Raul led the paramedics to Renee.

"Is everyone else alright?" Raul asked.

"Yes," I said.

Mr. Hines said, "You can come out now. The danger is over. Don't leave the house until you're given the all-clear."

Shelby asked, "Is everyone alright? Was anyone hurt?"

"Marc is dead; Maxine shot him. He was going to kill George. Now, Please," Mr. Hines said, "excuse me," as he exited the office. Raul and I stared at each other for a long moment. He left the house, as well. I sensed he had more to say.

The paramedics loaded Renee onto a Gurney. Shelby and I got into the ambulance.

"Dr. Mortimer will meet us at the hospital, Renee," I said.

Renee sighed, "He is an accomplished Doctor, and yet, Michael hated him. For a time, Dr. Mortimer tried to help Michael be a better man until Dr. Mortimer refused to be complicit or endure ongoing cruelty. Michael threw the Doctor aside for Raul, who would do anything for Michael – and did."

Renee was traumatized, sober, and talkative.

"I knew, you know," Renee said. "I have eyes and ears. I learned to live with trifles and stay happy. It's a talent, you know. From the beginning, I knew about George's penchant for Joanne's company. I saved him when I adopted Michael. Marc saved George by going to prison for his weaknesses. George had cases sealed. Promises were made, but George's promises weren't enough. They wanted more. I called the FBI when I suspected embezzlement. George didn't know I called. He will be angry with me."

We arrived at the hospital, and Renee was taken in through the ambulance entrance. I saw Morty greet the gurney as the doors closed. He looked at me and mouthed, "I'll take care of her."

I somehow trusted that Renee was in good hands. Renee was right. Morty was "a good man," despite his loyalty to ill-conceived associates and his crime of passion. Raul and Mr. Hines entered the ER lobby.

"George is on his way," Mr. Hines said. "He is saying goodbye to Maxine. She was arrested for manslaughter and mirandized. She is being questioned for her role in a scheme to embezzle George. George loved her."

Raul added, "And he believed she loved him."

"So did I," I said sadly and Shelby nodded.

Raul said, "Mr. Hines is part of the FBI team that infiltrated the track."

Mr. Hines announced, "We came to Merit to investigate the muddy waters of embezzlement. In the process, my team discovered an intricate system of manipulating race outcomes. We learned of the Mob's involvement and their connection to Michael, who tipped the scales for winners or losers. George's installation of security at the Estate was a deterrent but not 100% effective. George was guilty of many things but not involvement with the mob or racing fraud."

Raul said, "I am a cooperating witness and FBI informant."

I swallowed hard.

"Mr. Hines is my FBI contact."

I felt my blood pressure begin to climb. I felt no sympathy for Raul, but my contempt was turning to fear.

Raul said, "I am guilty of turning a blind eye to illegal activities and covering up crimes, faults, and folly. In return for my cooperation, I will remain an unindicted co-conspirator."

His gaze fell to the floor.

Mr. Hines spoke again, "Until Fran and Roger's murders, the FBI believed Michael was at the helm. Michael was involved in an array of illegal activities, including fraud, sex crimes, extortion, and tampering with government property. Raul was Michael's right arm. Once we arrested Raul and he agreed to cooperate, we were able to work faster. Unfortunately, not fast enough to prevent Roger or Fran's deaths, which we could not have foreseen. We were waiting for Michael to tip his hand and reveal with whom he was working." Raul's eyes met mine. Mr. Hines said, "Michael's untimely death threw us off the scent, temporarily, but Marc's activities and behavior were worth watching."

Mr. Hines told us that the FBI was surveilling Marc, and thanks to my meetings with the FBI, suspicions, and questions, Marc got nervous. He led them straight to Mitch Malcolm. Marc was the betrayed and the betrayer in his own saga.

Mr. Hines said, "Mitch was the kingpin behind a covert operation at the track that involved poisoning horses or disabling jockeys, manipulating odds, misrepresenting statistics in racing forms, extortion, and equipment tampering. He had Fran killed and paid Rosario to kill Roger. Mitch used Marc to access the Estate. Marc was the 'mule,' if you will, of the communication between Michael and Mitch. They never met face to face, never sent an e-mail or text, and never spoke on the phone. But it was Joanne and Marc, with Maxine's help, who embezzled the Candiss Estate Trust."

Emily entered the hospital. Mr. Hines explained that Emily was an FBI agent. He filled her in on the discussion. She reached out her hand.

"Agent Peters," she said.

Shelby and I shook her hand and dropped our jaws. "But we love you," Shelby said, "and you're such a good cook."

We laughed somewhat inappropriately. Emily informed us, "We knew that Joanne had leverage over George when we uncovered Judy and Michael's sealed adoptions. From there, we uncovered a tangled web of deceit. Joanne exploited Marc's hatred for George by persuading Marc to embezzle and betray George. They used George's relationship and reliance on Maxine to further their influence. They threatened to divulge the truth about George's sexual contact with young Joanne. Marc also threatened to harm Judy.

As the two FBI agents continued to share their story, it was clear that Joanne, for her own distorted reasons, encouraged Marc to solicit help from Maxine. Joanne wanted to break the bond between those two. Maxine kept George on the hook by pretending she was looking after Judy out of love for George. George was an innocent participant in Joanne's unparalleled quest for money, power, and revenge. For her part in the deceit, Joanne had promised Maxine a more prominent place in a financial future. Sex with George was easy in terms of what Maxine would stand to gain. She knew George would throw her away and move on with a younger woman someday. She would be left with nothing.

Mr. Hines said, "Mitch planted Fran in Judy's shop to give Marc access to Judy. Marc had information on Judy's schedules and whereabouts, as well as access to the Estate and Maxine."

Emily said, "The problems arose for Joanne when Marc became obsessed with Maxine. Marc couldn't stand how Maxine could please Mr. Candiss with her body. Marc held Mr. Candiss responsible for every misfortune Marc suffered throughout his life. Joanne's sexual relationship with Mr. C led to the seven-year incarceration and disruption of Marc's life. Marc paid another man's penance and was fueled by anger."

Mr. Hines added, "When Maxine rejected Marc's advances, Marc blamed Mr. C. Marc would have killed Mr. C tonight if Maxine had not shot and killed Marc as he knocked Mr. C. to the ground."

Chapter Thirty-Nine

Shelby and I stared wide-eyed at the group of FBI agents as the story was recounted. We were surprised and intrigued. As the details were shared silence fell over the group.

Shelby asked, "Why Gwen?" Tears filled her eyes.

Mr. Hines hesitated. Emily spoke up, "Gwen stumbled on a large discrepancy in The Candiss account and Trust. She thought it was a banking error. She mentioned it to Renee, who mentioned it to George in the limo.

Mr. Hines said, "Marc overheard and tried to delete the info online. Gwen had saved a file on her laptop and Marc wanted access. We think he tried to take the laptop from Gwen, but she wouldn't give it up. We believe the fall was the result of a struggle."

I put my arm around Shelby and pulled her close. Mr. Hines and Emily explained what occurred that night. It turns out that Marc did not come into the Estate through the gates. He came in on foot, over the wall, from the back of the Estate and took Mr. C's car from the garage. He drove back to the garage, left the car, and exited the Estate on foot again. He remotely deleted the exterior camera footage of his presence outside the main house. The FBI was able to recover that footage and were able to obtain arrest warrants for Marc and Joanne. The FBI was on their way to execute those warrants when they intercepted the 911 call about Gwen's accident.

Mr. Hines said, "We sat on our warrants to investigate Gwen's death. We became aware of Maxine's involvement when we explored Gwen's laptop. The questionable transactions were made by Maxine. Joanne was picked up tonight by an FBI team in Greely, Texas."

Dalton and George came quickly through the door with Agents Brent and Baxter. Dalton joined our group and the others went directly through the ER doors to see Renee. Dalton had blood on his shirt from a wound George sustained in his scuffle with Marc. Dalton was visibly shaken.

He said, "Marc is dead."

He realized we all knew. Dalton was unnerved as he scanned our faces.

"It's ok, now, Dalton," I said. "It's over."

Dalton took two steps back and sank into a chair in the lobby. Shelby and

I consoled him. Emily shook his hand.

"FBI," she said, "Agent Peters."

Dalton sat, aghast. "I am ready for a drink," he said.

"Me too!" Agent Peters responded.

Mr. Hines and Emily (Agent Peters) left the lobby to consult with the other agents and check on Renee's status. Shelby walked to the snack bar in the main hospital with Dalton to get us all the coffee. Raul and I stepped outside.

He said, "Mrs. Candiss, I need to tell you something. I am a cooperating witness for the federal government in return for my freedom. That includes telling them everything I know about every crime in which I was aware or involved." My knees went weak as I realized I would, in fact, be going to jail for the death of my husband. I was nodding at Raul, waiting for the words to fall from his mouth. He said, "If I do not see jail time, I see no reason for Morty to. . . do you understand what I am saying?" He asked.

I was holding my breath. Raul said, "Morty is a good man. The FBI needn't know that Morty and I drugged Michael. What good could possibly come from that? We've decided to let sleeping dogs lie. I won't be confessing all my sins, or all the sins of others," he said. "Morty and I are asking that you, remain silent. We want you to take this to the grave." His words trailed off. My heart was pounding against my ribs. He continued, "It was my idea for Morty to convince you that you were behind Michael's death, but you weren't. We planned it long before. You did nothing, Mrs. Candiss. We killed Michael. The only thing we didn't plan was Morty's enduring love for you. Don't you see, it was us?" Raul's eyes narrowed as he scanned my face for a response. I walked away to catch my breath.

I went inside, and Shelby handed me a white paper cup of coffee. She had already added the cream. She looked at me tenderly.

She said, "Dalton is fairly shook-up."

I looked at Dalton, who was holding his coffee cup with both hands and looking straight ahead.

"It's been a rough ride," I said, "kind of like that bull."

Dalton looked at me and forced a grin. "Yes, ma'am, I mean Carly – I feel like whoever is at the controls needs to let up. I can't hold on much longer. This has been too much."

"Just let go," I said, "and we'll all rest in the cushions for a little while, Ok?"

Shelby, Dalton, and I shared a group hug and sat quietly in each other's support. I rested my head on Dalton's shoulder and closed my eyes.

George entered the lobby with Dr. Mortimer.

"Renee is going to be fine," Dr. Mortimer said. "She is hard-headed." We all laughed nervously. "She has a few stitches in her forehead and a broken ankle. Otherwise, she is unscathed by an aggressive attack that could have been much worse."

George said, "Thank you Carly and Shelby for all you did for Renee."

"It was mostly Emily," I said.

"Yes, George, Emily was our hero," Shelby agreed.

"Then I must thank her too," George answered.

Dr. Mortimer told us he would keep Renee overnight, but she could come home in the morning. George said that he would stay at the hospital. He said, "It's the least I can do for poor Renee; I owe her. She tried to tell me, but I wouldn't listen. I thought her warning was just part of her ongoing feelings of distrust for Joanne and Maxine, although, I admit now, those too were warranted."

Dr. Mortimer took a hold of my hand. He kissed my cheek and looked deeply into my eyes. "Goodbye, Mrs. Candiss," he said, and he disappeared through the double doors leading to the ER. George followed close behind. I watched Morty go as sadness and relief filled my heart. Shelby interrupted my gaze by stepping in front of me.

"Carly, why don't you call Jonah? Dalton and I are going back to the Estate. We'll see you tomorrow."

I kissed them good night and settled back into the hard, plastic chair of the ER lobby. I reflected on Raul's disclosure and wondered why he admitted their crime. I realized he did it because of their peculiar, enmeshed love for one another. As dysfunctional as it was, he did it for Morty. Raul was right in the barn that night when he told me, "WE always end up together." I was and have been blind, naive, complicit, guilty, and innocent. I dialed Jonah's number.

George came into the waiting room and sat beside me. His face was covered in a shroud of remorse.

"She's asleep," he said. "Please forgive me, Carly. I have made many mistakes. I am a weak man."

I put my hand on George's knee, "I don't think it's my forgiveness you need, George."

He looked at the floor.

"I know," he said. "Poor Renee, how she has put up with me all these years is a mystery."

"The alcohol helped," I said.

George and I shared a moment of honesty through our gaze.

I said, "Isn't it incredible how convoluted life can become; what can become 'normal' and what we can adapt to?"

George nodded, "Can we ever make it right again?"

"I don't know. I only know we have to try," I said. "Sometimes, life gives us the opportunity to be better, and if it does, we need to try."

George nodded. He kissed me goodnight and went back into the ER to stay with Renee.

Jonah came through the ER doors like a madman. He took me in his arms and squeezed so tight I couldn't breathe. He lifted me off the ground.

"Oh, Carly," he said, "I am so glad you weren't hurt. How is Renee?" Jonah was breathless.

I calmed him down. "I am fine," I said. "I am not hurt. I am rattled, a little confused, and exhausted, but fine."

Jonah and I took two seats away from the others in the waiting room. He listened as I shared this evening's events and the information shared by the FBI. He was stricken with fear when he realized that Shelby and I interrupted Marc's assault on Renee.

"You could have been killed," he sighed.

He put his arms around me and held me in silence for a long moment. He loosened his embrace and sat back. Our eyes met.

"Marry me, Carly. Be my wife. I don't want to lose you, and now is the time to tell you – I love you; I love you."

I could feel his love at my core. My bones vibrated. My heart leaped. My mind raced. I could feel his love. This was real, true, pure and good.

He said, "I'll be the best partner I can be. I promise to be there for you, to take care of your mare, and rub your feet by the fire as often as possible."

I threw myself into Jonah's arms.

"Yes," I said, "Oh, yes."

We wiped tears from each other's cheeks.

Could this be happening? Was this real? Had the universe forgiven my sins? Could I be happy, cared for, and loved? Was it possible?

Made in the USA
Columbia, SC
07 November 2024